CROCUS BOOKS
no limits
URBAN SHORT STORIES

NO LIMITS

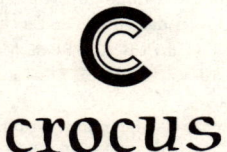

no limits
Urban short stories

First published in 1994 by Crocus

Crocus books are published by
Commonword Ltd,
Cheetwood House,
21 Newton Street,
Manchester M1 1FZ.

(c) Commonword Ltd and the authors.

No part of this publication may be reproduced without written permission, except in the case of brief extracts embodied in critical articles, reviews or lectures. For information contact Commonword Ltd.

Commonword gratefully acknowledges financial assistance from the Association of Greater Manchester Authorities, North West Arts Board and Manchester City Council.

Crocus Books are distributed by Password (Books) Ltd, 23 New Mount Street, Manchester M4 4DE.

Cover photography by Ruth Martin.
Cover design by Pao Lo Hu.
Produced by Pao Lo Hu 71 Bolton Road, Manchester M6 7HN
Printed by Shanleys, 16 Belvoir St., Tonge Fold, Bolton.

British Library Cataloguing-in-Publication Data.
A catalogue record for this book is available from the British Library.

Contents

Introduction	vii
Saturday Nightshift *Noel Hannan*	1
The Dragon on the Wall *Julie Farrand*	9
The Sheries *Qaisra Shahraz*	22
Jamie *Christopher B. Skyrme*	31
Legoland on Mescalin *Catriona Smith*	35
Queens' Court *José Gent*	45
Watching Wanting *Glenda Brassington*	49
Summer 1957 - Dream of the Desert *Valérie Olek*	56
Straight Grain *Julie Lerpiniere*	63
Mascara *Paul Morris*	73
The Visit *Fokkina McDonnel*	81
From Suceava, you can hear the Wolves *Sylvia Christie*	84
The Chalk Face *Valerie Clarke*	92
Size Twelve *Ailsa Cox*	98
Getting It *Helen Smith*	108
A Fish in the Sky *Pat Winslow*	114
Biographies	121

Introduction

Across the world people are drawn to the hectic diversity of city life – to the freedom and opportunities it affords. But beneath the frenetic exhilaration lurks a gritty reality of struggle and alienation.

No Limits is a collection of sixteen short stories by North West writers, who have skillfully captured the complex experience of urban living. Most of the writers have been published previously and some already have their foot firmly wedged in the literary door of fame, if not fortune. But what shines through most, in all their work, is a love of writing and a dedication to their craft. They write with honesty and sensitivity and are not afraid to tackle intimate or painful subjects.

A rich cast of characters, combined with crisp, incisive and often witty writing makes *No Limits* a liberating read. This urban travelogue will take you from present day Lahore to twenty-first century Manchester and beyond. We hope you enjoy the journey.

Sincere thanks to Tom Barclay and Qaisra Shahraz for their work on the editing panel.

Cathy Bolton
Commonword Ltd.

Saturday Nightshift

Noel Hannan

The alarm clock wakes me gently, just as I like it. It casts its watery hologram against the whitewashed far wall and murmurs with its insistent voice

ninepmtimetogetupninepmtimetogetupninepm

I crawl out of bed and search for something fairly clean to wear among the jumble on the floor. I find a pair of graphite leggings and a black bra that don't smell too bad, so they'll do.
The pinkbluegreen neon slices in through the horizontal blinds. I pull the cord and the room is illuminated by the huge Sony graphicsboard mounted on the apartment block on the street corner. I've lived in this flat for two years and I've never owned a light bulb. Thank you, Sony.
I love to watch the city
(my city)
at night. It's raining, a mild drizzle that does little to dissipate the omnipresent heat but turns the landscape into an entertaining kaleidoscope. Neon and graphics reach up as far as the eye can see, climbing to heaven on the flanks of blind skyscrapers, and plunge down into the fathomless depths of hell, all perspective lost in the mirrored, rain-slicked streets. Then oil mixes with water and turns the city
(my city)
into a bad hallucinogenic vision.
I've little more than an hour to go before I have to be at work, but there's *always* time to watch some TV. I switch on the Amstrad Multiscreen in the corner, a forty-inch beast that lets me watch eight channels simultaneously. I would've liked the sixteen-screen version but this was the best I could afford. It's still the most expensive thing I own. I sit and channel-flip for a while.
News on channel eighteen. The civil war rages on in

Europe. I take a mild interest as I'm due to be conscripted next year. It pays to know who it is you're supposed to be fighting. Apparently, Luxembourg has fallen to the Turko-Serbian-Slovak Alliance and there has been another nuclear attack on Athens. Elsewhere, the US shuttle Colombus is in orbit around Mars, preparing to send down the first manned exploration vessel. Good luck to 'em, I say.

I tire at current events pretty easily, and look for some game shows. Russian Roulette is on, my favourite, so I slip a blank disc into the recorder and set it going. I can watch it when I get back from work. In the corner of the screen, the home shopping channel intersperses its advert for a fruit juice machine with subliminal shots of a hot summer beach, each one-tenth of a second and barely visible. But I know that they're there and I reckon you'd have to be brain dead not to see them. Prime time TV for rehabilitating junkies. Who sunbathes these days anyway? Nobody, if they don't want skin cancer. Come to think of it, I do feel kind of thirsty.

Time to go. Joe Takei won't be impressed if I'm late again, and I need the money from this job to keep the flat. I've no wish to be out on the streets again, no thank you.

As I struggle into my Goretex smock and dig through discarded clothes for my cycling helmet and mask, something catches my eye through the window on the vast civic graphicsboard downtown, a blaze of colour and light that overwhelms even the Sony board no more than a street's width from me. The civic board, in an impressive scrolling array of animation, trumpets the start of the game playoffs, sponsored by Nintendo, for the World Supreme Champion. The contestants are Duane Kasparov (CSI) and Kylie Manotova (Australasia Pacific Rim Conurb). The prize is a Caribbean island. Images of the game players appear on the screen – androgynous, withered things with bloated heads, bug eyes and overdeveloped hands. Kylie has had her eyelids removed so she doesn't blink. Her camp reckon it is a championship-winning strategy.

I'd love to be the World Champion, but to sacrifice your body, even for a Caribbean island of your very own? No thanks. I like my body and there are other people who appreciate it too. Reminded of this, I do a few callisthenics to limber up. I add a couple of exercises for my game-playing fingers too. Just in case.

I've got my helmet on now, and my mask hangs from it by a press stud. I delve beneath my mattress and take out my gunbelt. It contains two pistols, set up for a cross draw, and they hang low on my hips, clear of the smock's hem. I use a .357 Magnum Colt Python and a Desert Eagle automatic in the same calibre. I appreciate the stopping power of the .357, invaluable when some crazy high on crack is intent on making you make his day, and having both guns chambered for it means I can swap ammo if one gun jams. The wheel gun is my insurance policy - revolvers are practically foolproof. All the coppers are armed with them. But it only takes six shots and sometimes you need the extra capacity of the Eagle which takes thirteen. The best of both worlds.

I'm now protected against the hostile environment of the city
(my city)
and I'm going to be late if I don't get a move on. I leave the flat in its permanent state of chaos, the Multiscreen babbling to itself in the corner to fool any would-be intruder that I'm home, I've had a bad day, I'm cleaning my guns at the kitchen table and it wouldn't be a good idea to piss about with me. Not tonight.

The door slides shut on hydraulic rams behind me. Later, when I return, an eyesafe laser will scan my retina for identification before I can get back in.

What? Paranoid? Are you kidding? You obviously don't live in this city, any city
(my city)

My mountain bike is chained to the stairway below with enough metal to sink Houdini. It's another of my prize possessions, a lightweight proto-alloy model from Muddy Paw, with an automatic Shimano transmission powered by a rechargeable NiCad pack. Integral lights and nylon-reinforced tyres. Jet black. Very sleek.

The usual Saturday night crowd are on the street. Pimps, hookers, pushers, gangsters, mobsters, plain-clothes coppers (sticking out like bulldogs' bollocks, nervous seventeen year olds far too clean-shaven for their technicolour ravewear), street vendors and posers. But it's a dangerous district downtown if you're not a native. An item of clothing, an inflection of speech, an accidental look can bring sudden violence. Still they come from uptown and the suburbs to see what all the fuss is about. Goddamn tourists. Maybe it would have been better for all of us if they *had* declared martial law. At least then we would know who to shoot at.

I keep my head down and keep pedalling through the rainslick streets. It's stopped raining and there's little traffic apart from the (very) occasional police cruiser, windows up and travelling at high speed. They think of downtown as a safari park and we're the monkeys and tigers. Don't stop at the junction, copper, or we'll rip your windscreen wipers off. If you're lucky.

The nightlife spills from the pavements and dominates the abandoned streets. I veer and chicane through drunken revellers and sullen-faced street dwellers. I see familiar faces from my own time as a scavenger and street-survivor. Some of them were friends, but not any more. To be a survivor, you have to rise to the top of the heap, float on the scum pile until you get a chance to jump off. I did some nasty things to get off the street and there are no doubt debts still to be paid. I'm far from ready to honour some of them. If some of my 'friends' knew that I had an apartment and a job, they would not think twice before removing my eyeball with fingers and using it to fool the ID laser, and steal everything I've worked so hard for. I've not been away from the street for long enough to make new friends who might protect me from such an eventuality.

But I do have a brother. His name is Marty, and here he is on a street corner, striking a deal. I pull up short on the kerb twenty metres away and watch him. He's only fourteen but he's already got hoods twice his age working for him. I wonder why he's down here on the streets, putting himself in danger when his footsoldiers should be doing this for him.

He looks nervous even from this distance, shifting from foot to foot and taking swift, shallow pulls on a skinny reefer. His clients, two black and one white youth in

Halcyon Turf sportswear, are examining the packages he has handed to them. There are loud exchanges and contorted faces and my gut knots as I realise something is going to happen.

The packages are hurled to the floor at Marty's feet and split open, spilling white powder into the gutter and puddles. Marty reaches inside the green padded flight jacket he always wears. I reach for my guns too in an instinctively protective movement but realise they are too far away for me to back Marty up without fear of hitting him.

The youths backpedal, hands scrabbling for concealed weapons, but Marty already has the Uzi up in the aim and is cocking it with his left hand. The muggy night air is split with a thunderclap and my retinas burn with the muzzle flash. Marty hoses the Uzi left-right and the three youths go down as if the world has just collapsed on to their shoulders.

Marty stops shooting and the street is filled with false silence from buzzing ears. Marty, oh so cool, looks over his shoulder at the street people emerging sheepishly from behind dumpsters and storefronts, deposits the Uzi back in his shoulder holster and runs from the scene.

I follow. I'm much faster on the Muddy Paw than even Marty's long-legged stride, but he starts to duck and dive down alleys and back entrances. I stop at the mouth of one and unclip my mask, hoping he'll recognise me. Marty is a shadowplay puppet at the other end.

'Marty!' I shout. He stops and I see him turn, the Uzi in his hand again and rising into the aim. My blood chills in my veins.

'Marty! It's me, Luisa!'

The muzzle drops sharply and I breathe again. He makes his way down the alley toward me. The Uzi is still in his hand, hanging at his side.

'Luisa,' he says, giving me one of his brief cursory hugs that pass for his version of brotherly love. 'I nearly popped you. What are you doing here?'

'I'm on my way to work,' I say. 'I saw what happened. What's the matter, can't your hired guns be trusted to cut deals on the street anymore?'

He grimaces and for a moment looks very much like the little boy he really is. My little brother.

'A miscalculation, Luisa.' He makes a shrug that implies cynicism way beyond his years. He's a hood leader again. 'The Halycon Turf insisted on dealing face to face. Now I know why. It was a mob hit. I think they were hired by the Snugbury Close Family. Or maybe the coppers. We'll see.'

Sirens interrupt us, the piercing rise and fall of the cop cruisers mixed and dubbed with the wail of an ambulance. Marty stiffens and noses the air like a retrieving hound.

'I got to go, Luisa. Take care. Stay out of trouble. You know how to find me if you need me.' He pecks my cheek and for a moment the Uzi is a dead weight against my thigh, like an unexpected erection. Then he's gone.

I pedal back through the litter-strewn alleys to the burning neon of the main street. It is a carnival of sound and light, police cruisers and ambulances slamming to a halt at aggressive angles, and body-armoured police assembling into a riot phalanx. The people turn their music up several notches, as they always do when the police are around in force. The effect is overwhelming. The sounds of loop-rhythms, pulsing baselines and tortured electric guitars combine to hinder the coppers' concentration. In desperation, they call for the big boys and soon a tank is nosing its way down the street, amber emergency lights strobing and its big gun tracking across the storefronts.

Downtown is in uproar, a usual Saturday night. Animosity develops through fistfights into knifefights, knifefights into gun battles, and gun battles into turf war, all fuelled by long - standing hatreds and alcohol and drug consumption.

My city is a war zone.
(my city)

My place of work is at the end of the main street, a ground floor unit fronted by a huge plate glass window that gets protected by an armoured screen out of business hours. There's an alley to one side and it leads around the back to the tradesmen's entrance. And the kitchen.

'Where's you been?' Joe Takei roars, as I chain up my

bike in the litter-strewn yard. He's standing in the kitchen doorway and he's got a filthy apron tied over his business suit. He's the fattest Japanese man I know. He's elbowed to one side by Davy coming out of the kitchen, shrugging into a Goretex smock like my own.

'Good luck kid.' Davy winks at me. 'He's in a foul mood tonight.'

Davy's my shift partner on Tuesdays and Thursdays but tonight he's pulled an early shift. He unlocks his own bike and rides off down the alley, giving Takei the finger once he's out of view.

'You five minutes late,' Takei blusters, pulling off the apron. 'This your job, not mine. I dock your pay.'

'I'm coming, Joe,' I say, snatching the apron from Takei's grip. He's all wind and importance and I don't take him too seriously. He pinches my arse too often for comfort and I'm hoping I can keep my job without having to let him fuck me. He *can't* dock my pay - I'm working a whole hour for five days a week and it's just enough to keep the flat and keep me fed. I can't *afford* to have my pay docked. Maybe Takei will get what he wants in the end.

Joe Takei's is a Sushi-bar. The sign above the door reads EST. 1998. 25 YEARS THE FINEST SUSHI IN MANCHESTER

I prepare fish for the meals and also for the display in the window, which features live fish. I have to hold a fish down on the marble slab and scoop the flesh from each of its flanks in turn, from gill to tail, with a razorsharp filleting knife. The fish continues to flip and flop for some time. I place them in the window with the raw vegetable and flower arrangements. Every few hours I have to replace them with fresh ones.

I steal a glance through the swing doors as I start work. There's a party of twenty or so suited businessmen and their wives from Cheshire, laughing loudly and spilling wine on the tables. They've probably been helicoptered in tonight to get a taste of the authentic inner city. Later, after their meal and a tour downtown in armoured limos with police escorts, they'll fly back to their cosy secure estates in the countryside with their razor wire and rottweilers, and the men will be too pissed to fuck and the women won't care. They'll fall asleep thinking, hoping, that none of the zoo animals they've seen tonight feel like repaying the compliment and visiting them.

I push my filleting knife into a fish's gill. It struggles. They say fish have no nervous system. Sometimes I feel we have none too.

Takei moves smugly among the surbanites, who ignore him. He increases the polarity on the glass window to shield them from a group of beggars who have taken up station outside. I know in a minute he's going to get me to move them on.

Perhaps Takei's customers would like to take my tour of the city,
 (my city)
a city with no nervous system, a city immune to shock, a city where everyone and everything is your enemy.

My city.
 (my city)
 (my city is a war zone)

The Dragon on the Wall (For Jeanne)

Julie Farrand

Some squatters have moved into the house at the back of mine. The bedroom windows have been broken for a long time, but this morning I noticed that two of them have been boarded up where the glass was missing. It's going to be very cold at nights when the winter comes round. If they're still there. People come and go in this neighbourhood.

I'm not sure how many of them are living there, but I saw a woman moving about the back room while I was making a cup of tea in the kitchen. I could see a TV set flickering, but I don't think there's much else in there.

A bit later on I saw a little boy come running out of the back door. The woman was shouting after him, 'I want you back in half an hour Marlon, do you hear me?'. Marlon didn't give her a backward glance; just jumped over a pile of bricks, and then I lost sight of him as he ran down the entry.

It's a wasteland out there. Full of bin liners that have been ripped apart by the dogs, and all the rubbish spilling out onto the cobbles. I had a go at clearing it up once. I found a syringe lying on the ground underneath a pile of rusty cans and decaying food. I imagined somebody creeping along there late at night and shooting up in the darkness outside my back gate. It gave me the shivers, so I left it all to carry on mouldering.

* * *

The weather has been very warm just recently. It makes everyone lazy and even the dust doesn't move about like it usually does. I sit out on the steps by the back door when it's nice, and get a bit of sun. It really catches it in the yard in the afternoons. I had some pansies in a tub by the gate, but the cats dug them up and pissed in the pots. There aren't many trees or flowers around here. Only the rubbish blooms in the spring, and you catch a waft of it when the breeze is blowing. Some days I feel as if I've been fossilised in a layer of dirt.

I hear the voice of the city in the summertime. The noise is carried on the back of the heat that hangs over the streets and the rooftops. It's raucous and loud and drags people out of their houses to sit in the back yards and on the front door steps. I hear them talking above the sound of the music on the radios blaring from kitchens and living rooms.

I was listening to its song late this afternoon, and wondering when it would call me back again, when I saw the little boy for the second time. He had climbed up over my back wall and perched on top of it like a victorious mountain climber. He was wearing a pair of khaki pants and a matching shirt that hung down loosely over his skinny wrists. His features were small and indistinct, as if they were trying to escape from the expression on his face. I couldn't see the colour of his eyes, but I guessed they would be flat and grey, like a muddy pool of water. I said, 'You shouldn't be up there, you'll break your neck.'

'No I won't,' he said, kind of surly.

'Oh yes you will,' I said.

I'm not very good with children. Never having had any. So I let him sit up there. He looked sure enough. He was playing with some kind of toy, or little statue, and I asked him what it was. I could see it was brightly coloured – blue and violet and green – but I couldn't make out what it was from where I was sitting.

He told me it was a dragon. I asked him what sort of dragon and he looked at me like I was stupid, and said, 'the dragon on the wall'.

We ignored each other quite happily for about half an hour, and he left when his mum called him in for tea. I went inside too. It's Monday, and I go to my group meeting on a Monday.

I've been going there for about six months now. It's up at St. Mary's in town, in a side room off the corridor in the Psychiatric Unit. I think it's doing me good, although it's hard to measure your own progress.

They say I need to get out more and stop cutting myself

off from things. But the summer makes me lazy and I just like to sit and watch sometimes. Time passes by me, unmarked, except for mealtimes, and the occasional walk, or a trip to the library. I'm building myself up for the day I feel strong enough to go out and live again. It can get lonely.

I use the time to listen, and think, and feel.

* * *

I thought somebody was out in my back yard last night. I could hear this noise like someone trying to dig through rock with a spade. It woke me up. I keep an iron bar by the bed, though God knows what use it would be if somebody broke in, armed and dangerous. I crept in the back bedroom that overlooks the yard, but I couldn't see anything at first. Just heard this scraping noise. Then I saw a dark shape moving about near the back door of the squatters' house, and it was banging a spoon or something, in time to music that I couldn't hear. Their back door was half open, and a light was on, but I couldn't make out anybody inside. I think it was Marlon. I wondered what he was doing out there by himself so late. I suppose it's none of my business.

There's a man living there now as well. I can hear him shouting and banging about at all times of the day and night. He calls to somebody called 'Cath', (it must be the woman) and he's always complaining about something. 'Where's my fucking shoes, Cath?' and, 'Mind what you're doing, you little twat,' (that must be Marlon.) She doesn't say anything back though. Or if she does, it's very quietly spoken.

Marlon came and sat on the wall again today. He had his dragon with him. It's quite big, about the size of a coffee mug, and I think he talks to it. His lips move, but no sound comes out. I asked him what it was called, but he ignored me. I tried a different tack.

'Have you been to school today?'
'Don't go to school.'
'Aren't you old enough?' I asked. He looks old enough. He shut up again and started talking to the dragon. I

wanted to talk some more, but he closed in on himself and I couldn't reach him there. He reminds me of a shadow, he's so quiet and motionless. It's as if I conjure him up from nowhere, and I wondered if he would exist without me here.

I gave the dragon a name anyway. I called it Fafnir, after a poem I read once. It's about a dragon who's just minding his own business and getting on with things.

But eventually the knights will come.

* * *

I've been feeling restless lately. Perhaps I'm getting tired of doing nothing. The city is sleeping today under the hot sun, but it still cries out like it's having a bad dream, and it makes me feel strange. As if I want to do something. But I don't know what.

The man across the way was making a terrible row this evening. Cath shouted back at him this time, and I heard crockery breaking and Marlon screaming. I was having my dinner, but I couldn't finish it because I lost my appetite. It unsettled me, and I felt as if something were being forced on me that I didn't want to have.

I went and sat out on the steps after I'd done the washing up, to have a cigarette and watch the day burn itself out. I took my book with me and became engrossed in it, so I didn't notice when the back gate started to creak open. When I looked up, Marlon was standing in front of me holding Fafnir in his hands. The dragon's head had become dislocated from his body somehow, and he looked pretty sorry for himself. Well, they both did; Marlon and the dragon.

'Hello,' I said, putting the book down. 'What happened to Fafnir?'

He looked blank. Of course, I forgot, he doesn't know his name.

I tried again.

'What happened to the Dragon?'

'It got broke, didn't it.'

I had some superglue in the kitchen cupboard so I leant forward to take his toy off him, to see if it could be mended.

He jumped away like I'd tried to hit him, and glared at me.

'It's not yours, it's mine. And it's broke.'

'I can see that,' I said. 'Give it here and I'll try and mend it for you.'

His face was really quite dirty and there were tear tracks all the way down his cheeks, coursing through the muck. His clothes weren't much better. He looked like he'd spent the day on a scrap heap.

He handed the dragon over to me reluctantly, and I took it inside and read the instructions on the tube of glue. I could see Marlon out of the corner of my eye, edging his way nearer the door, but I didn't turn round. He reminded me of a little bird, hopping nearer, then getting ready to fly away again. I held my breath and concentrated on what I was doing, frightened that if I made a sudden move he would run away. After a few minutes I said, 'you can come in if you want to. Would you like something to drink?'

He sat down on the top step and nodded his head up and down without looking at me, so I poured him a cupful of lemonade and set it down beside him.

Fafnir's head had broken off quite cleanly and it didn't look like he'd suffered any permanent damage. He really was gross though. Whoever had painted him must have been under the influence, because the colours all ran together and, close up, he looked pretty sad.

I poured myself a lemonade and left the dragon on the worktop to gel. Marlon was drinking his like he'd never had a drink before.

'Are you thirsty?' I asked, to break the awkward silence.

'Is he going to be alright then?' he asked.

I felt like Doctor Kildare with the power of life and death, and the silly thought made me laugh. I haven't laughed for a long time. It bubbled up in my throat and came out as a kind of hiccup, so I busied myself with the lemonade to disguise it.

'Yes, he should be okay. Why don't you come back later and get him, if your mum says it's okay.'

'Mum's not in. She's gone to our Jackie's.'

'Ask your Dad then.'

He gave me an old-fashioned look and started playing with a button on his shirt.

'I haven't got a Dad. And anyway, I'm not asking him nothing.'

And then he got up and walked out of the yard with his hands in his pockets and his head tilted back at an unmentionable angle. I started to call him back, but my voice trailed off into silence. I was annoyed with myself for saying the wrong things and, for some reason that I didn't really understand, I wanted to cry.

Later that night I did cry. Great dry, heaving sobs, that came crashing out of me and breaking into the room. The sound of my own misery echoed back from the walls and made me cry even harder. Afterwards I felt dry and empty and small, curled up underneath the bedcovers. I slept deeply without dreaming.

* * *

Last night at the Group I told them about Marlon, and the dragon getting broken. I'm not sure why. They asked me what I thought it meant to me. I said I didn't think it meant anything really. I just felt sorry for the kid. I sensed that they didn't quite believe me and I knew I was keeping something back. But whether it was pity for myself, or for Marlon, I didn't know.

Instead, I talked some more about the time before I went into hospital. How one day I decided to stay in bed and not get up again until the bad feeling had gone away. But it didn't go away. It settled in a corner of the room and glared at me through the smoke from endless cigarettes, willing me to give in, so that it could climb into bed with me and wrap the sheets around our heads.

* * *

Marlon called round this afternoon to pick up the dragon. It's been sitting on the worktop for three days and we've become quite friendly. I talk to him out loud, and I kind of miss having a real person to share a conversation with. My voice sounded rusty, but quite pleasant. Shame there was only a dragon's deaf ears for it to fall upon. I found a packet of unopened chocolate humbugs in the larder and I shared them with Marlon out in the back yard. He seemed pleased to have Fafnir back and he inspected him carefully to see if he could find the join. Then, with the air of someone making a great and important announcement, he told me that he was going to go to school and his mum was going to buy him lots of new clothes and a bike to go to school on. The words came tumbling out one after another, falling over themselves in their hurry to escape. I was so carried away by his enthusiasm, I could almost see him pedalling down Stockport Road like a fury, on his way to school. The child in me responded to this, but the adult knew it was unlikely to happen.

He asked me what I did, and whether I went to school. I told him I used to, but that was a long time ago, and I didn't do anything very much at the moment. He looked puzzled and went very thoughtful for a while, then he said,'you can play with my soldier if you want,' and pulled this tatty little plastic soldier out of his pocket and dumped it in my lap. I said 'thank you very much' and twisted the arms about a little bit, and made 'bang bang' noises. Marlon laughed and I was gratified. Children are much easier to amuse than adults.

He asked me what my name was and when I told him, I was surprised to find that it still belonged to me. Then I told him the story about Fafnir and the Knights, and he said he liked it and the dragon didn't deserve to get his head kicked in. I agreed. He stayed with me until tea time and then went home. I remained outside for a while, soaking up the last of the afternoon sun, before going back indoors again.

The summer is really getting underway, and some nights I can hardly sleep for the heat. I lie naked underneath the single sheet, and think about the past. The city is still singing to me, but the voice has a siren sound to it. I ignore the football chants at closing time and listen instead to the rattle of the trains as they tear through the night, and send it spinning. Slowly and carefully I go back in memory over the past six months, and examine them, the way you would a bruised limb, for signs of a healing process. When I first came out of hospital, in the middle of winter, the world felt as black and brittle as the sleeping branches of the trees. But the summer forces itself into my consciousness, and I feel something stirring.

* * *

I went into the city centre today to look round the shops. I'd forgotten how many people there were in the world. I was pushed down Market Street by the pressure of numbers and, every time I tried to walk alone, following the future of my own footsteps, somebody forced me into another path. There was a busker outside The Royal Exchange, playing the blues, and I stopped to listen for a while. Every shop doorway seemed to have music coming from it and I adjusted my pace every few seconds to accommodate the changing beat. The noise was pulling me towards it and, rather than feeling afraid I took it inside of me and we moved in time together.

I didn't go into any of the shops but, as I passed the windows, I caught sight of my own reflection looking back at me with an expression of recognition on its face.

I stopped off at a flower stall on the way to the bus station and bought a bunch of red roses, and inhaled their perfume all the way home. I hoped that Marlon would be there when I got back and, with this in mind, I started to make up a story about my day out. It had all the elements of a great adventure and in my imagination it became one.

When I got back, Marlon was sitting on the wall, playing with Fafnir. I was pleased to see him and I went straight out into the back yard to show him the roses. He wasn't very interested. The tell-tale marks were on his cheeks and I could see he'd been crying again . For a moment, I felt disappointed and let down, but I threw the thought away and asked him what the matter was.

He didn't reply. Instead, he began to bang the dragon's snout rather viciously against the wall. I lifted up my arms to help him down, and he didn't resist. He stood in front of me, silently looking at his feet, as if he'd never noticed them before. I asked him again, 'Is something up?'

'Mum's not very well, and I've got to stay and look after the house – he said so.'

'Who's he?' I said. But I knew who it was before he replied.

'Are you all by yourself then?' I asked.

He began to sniffle and said, in between deep breaths, 'Mum's gone to the hospital, 'cause she hurt her head, 'cause she fell down, and Steve told me to shut up and get out, and then the ambulance came and took her away.'

I didn't quite know what to make of all this and I was at a loss for the right thing to say. I felt slightly sick with worry and I chewed at the skin around my fingernails while I was thinking.

'What about Jackie, can't you go to Jackie's?'

I remembered the name, but didn't have a clue who she was. He didn't say anything. Just stroked Fafnir with his grubby little fingers as if it were a magic charm and he could fly away on the dragon's unsuitable back.

Without thinking about it any longer, I took him inside and switched the TV on. I left him in front of it, watching scenes of mayhem and murder on the Six O'Clock News, while I searched through the freezer for fishfingers or beefburgers.

I lit a cigarette and smoked it all the way down to the filter, while the burgers turned to brown leather and the chips burnt themselves to death in the pan. My kitchen had suddenly come alive with the sounds of activity that was no longer just for me. I wished I had the power to put his small universe in some sort of order, but all I could really do was cook him his tea.

After tea, we watched the television together. He sat there, hardly blinking, and I couldn't imagine that the words and the pictures made much impression on him. He was just like a sponge, soaking it all in and giving nothing out. I tried to talk to him, but he only replied in monosyllables. I continued to reassure him, saying that everything would be alright and his mum would be back soon. It didn't sound very reassuring, even to me and, after a while, I gave up and sat back and stared at the TV, without really taking any of it in.

About seven o'clock, I heard Steve shouting Marlon's

name from their back door. I told Marlon to stay where he was for a moment, and I walked across the entry and into their back yard. I'd never seen him up close before. He wasn't very old. Maybe twenty-two, but no more. He looked like a little terrier dog, and he made me slightly nervous, even though I was bigger than him.

'I've got Marlon at my house, if that's who you're looking for.'

He hadn't seen me come into the yard and I startled him. I saw an expression of distrust sweep across his face for a fleeting second and then he smiled at me. He had a front tooth missing and it made him look like the grotesque caricature of a naughty child.

'Well thanks a lot, love, but his mum's back now and she wants to know where he is.'

I asked rather weakly, 'Is she alright?'

'Oh she's fine, love,' he said. 'Just gave her head a bang falling up the stairs. If you want to bring Marlon out, I won't be troubling you anymore, love.'

I cringed when he called me love, and I disliked him more intensely than I had his voice. Marlon was fiddling with the buttons on the TV when I came back in, switching the channels backwards and forwards. I told him Steve was calling for him and it was time to go home now. I thought he might cry or refuse to leave, but his face was still blank and closed in on its thoughts. He just said, 'Yeah, okay, I'll go now then,' in a way that sounded far too grown up for his age.

I decided to have one more try, and I knelt down beside him and took his hands in mine saying, 'You will be okay, won't you, Marlon? You can always come and see me if you need me. I'll be here.'

The words sounded meaningless. Like a patchwork quilt that's been tacked together with no sense behind it. He twisted his head to one side, disentangled his fingers from mine and moved back a step. On an impulse, I reached across and patted his cheek just once, and very slightly. He didn't move or say anything, he just stared at me, and the expression on his face reminded me of the horror of an animal caught in a trap. I felt as if a wall had come down between us and we were facing each other across a wasteland of bricks and dirt. I didn't want to let him go back there to the house, but he moved away and walked towards the back door with me following behind him. When he got to the gate, he turned around and said 'Thanks for the tea. I liked the chips,' and disappeared down the entry, out of sight. I felt like a traitor handing a fellow countryman over to the enemy.

* * *

I was woken up this morning by a terrible screaming and shouting coming from across the way. I recognised their voices at once and I lay there tense, waiting to hear the sounds of breaking crockery again. This time Cath was shouting too, and I could hear her saying quite clearly, 'Fuck off you Bastard! Fuck off and leave us alone.'

Then I heard a car door slamming and somebody was banging on their back door. It was barely light and the birds had just started to cough their way into the dawn chorus, but they had fierce competition. The noise terrified me and I buried my head underneath the pillow, wishing I could stay there for good. I turned the radio on loud to drown out the noise and, by the time I turned it off again, it had all gone quiet, except for the hum of traffic on Stockport Road. The city was on its way to work again and coming to life with the creaks and groans of a great engine.

I slept in late, but eventually had to get up because the sun was forcing its way through the curtains with strong arms and heavy kicks. I stumbled downstairs in a sleep-induced daze and plugged the kettle in to make some tea. I made myself some toast, but it went cold while I stood looking out of the kitchen window, trying to see signs of life across the way.

I tried to visualise myself going across to their house, hammering on the back door and demanding to speak to Cath. I would tell her what I thought of Steve and make her take Marlon away from here, anywhere away from that man. I became a mythical hero, standing up for Good and Right, and killing the knights before they came to slay the dragons. My thoughts were fuelled by anger and sadness, but I knew my position was hopeless and there was really nothing that I could do to help.

And then I noticed something sitting on top of the wall. At first, I couldn't see what it was because the sun was in my eyes but, when I moved slightly, I saw Fafnir quietly basking in the sunshine and glowing green, violet, and blue.

I left him there all day and kept myself busy sweeping up the back yard and cleaning the house. Every so often, I went and stood at the gate and looked across at the house, but the back door stayed shut and everything was silent.

It was dark by the time I realised that Marlon wasn't going to show up. I went back inside and switched the TV on, and felt comforted by the babble of unfamiliar voices, although I hardly listened to a word of it.

* * *

I never saw him again. I saw Steve a couple of times, going in and out of the house, but Cath and Marlon must have left the morning that I heard the shouting and screaming. I found myself watching out for him and expecting to see him appear again in the back yard. And, even when I realised he wouldn't be coming back, my eyes would still be drawn to the top of the wall. After a couple of weeks, Steve disappeared as well, and there was no longer anything to interest me when I looked out of my kitchen window.

I brought the dragon inside and put him on the mantelpiece in the front room. He reminds me of how easy it is to get lost in the city, and I think of Marlon's dragon as a very fragile thing. The part of us that gets torn up and twisted by violence. I like to think he left the dragon for me to find. But more likely, it got left behind when they went in such a hurry. Either way it doesn't matter. I take care of it and make sure it doesn't get broken again.

The voice that calls to me sings about life and death, and destruction, and fear and hope. I hear it more and more often now, and louder. It won't be silenced. The trains and the cars and the radios and the people out on the steps are calling to me, and shaking the walls of the house. Soon the walls will crumble and I will   become a part of the city again.

Some older kids came round one day and put all the windows in. I was out there too late to stop them, but it didn't really matter anyway. The broken glass joined the pile of bricks and old carpet that was already out there, and they settled into the ground together.

The Sheries: City Dwellers

Qaisra Shahraz

Sher Khan got on the bus from his village, heading for the city of Lahore. Almost all of the village had come to see him off, out of respect – the men, women and children. He was a *busurgh*, one of the two remaining village elders. The children ran alongside him and offered *salam*. The young women, who he treated as his own daughters, ducked their covered head in front of him out of respect so that he could pat them on the head, as was the custom for an elder *busurgh*.

As he sat on the bus his self respect and dignity was never higher. The young men had helped him with his *ghitries*, his three parcels, onto the bus. The three parcels were presents, mainly home grown vegetables and pastries for his two life-long friends, who were now settled in Lahore, a large teeming city, once the capital of Pakistan and the home of the Mughal emperors.

Sher Khan was looking forward to meeting his two friends. He had spent his childhood, youth and most of his adult life with these two friends in the village. This was the first time he was going to visit them since they had left almost a decade ago. The friends had often visited him in the village. He always offered his home and his hospitality whenever they visited.

He was dressed in his best, crisply starched clothes which his daughter-in-law had prepared for him. He donned his *pagh*, his special turban, on his head and had dyed his white hair and beard with henna and trimmed his moustache.

The journey on the bus was a lonely one. He wished that he had brought his wife with him. The coach reached Lahore on time. It was almost evening. Sher Khan, struggling to hold his three parcels, got off the coach. He hadn't realised how heavy they were. There was always someone to carry things for him, so had never carried anything before. The village lads had carried them for him.

Now he stood on the pavement with two of them on the ground near to his feet and one in his arm. The hustle and bustle of the city disconcerted him. The traffic, the people, the buildings, and the anonymity of it all. Nobody knew him and nobody was going to rush to help him with his parcels. He anxiously rummaged through the pocket of his jacket to find the paper with the address of his two friends. The paper was still there and he felt himself sigh with relief.

Seeing a taxi, he waved it to stop, and the driver helped him into it. As he neared his destination, Sher Khan remembered that he had not written to his friends to tell them he was visiting them. He hoped that they didn't mind his coming out of the blue like this, but they never wrote to him when they came. He recalled his own and his family's pleasure at receiving guests no matter on which day or at what time they arrived, so he assumed that his friend and his family were the same. As the taxi wove through the maze of small streets and bazaars, exuding different smells of the city, Sher Khan almost felt nostalgic. He missed the clean, fresh air of his village fields. Here, it was a crowded scene, verging on almost a slum. Houses and living quarters were packed into one another. He wasn't sure where one accommodation started and another ended. The lanes were teeming with life, with people and traffic. Eventually the taxi drew to a halt and the driver pointed to a small building. It was a shop. Sher Khan looked at it, confused. His friend hadn't told him that it was a shop.

'Are you sure, young man, that this is the right place?'

'Oh yes,' replied the driver, 'there is the number. The people you want probably live above the shop. You go up those stairs.' Sher Khan spotted the two concrete steps leading to a door and, with the driver helping him with his parcels, he stepped out.

As the taxi drove away, Sher Khan looked around helplessly. How was he going to take his parcels up? He summoned the courage to call to the shop vendor nearby, selling make-up and toiletries, and asked if he would allow his young assistant to help him. The man obliged quickly.

'Yes, of course, *Baba jee*.' He answered using the respectful term for an old man. Sher Khan's face brightened at the man's answer. The young man came and lifted the three parcels effortlessly.

Together they climbed the steps and went through the door to more stairs, which they climbed to the top, to find themselves in a dark hallway. Sher Khan knocked on the door.

'You should have rung the bell, *Baba jee*,' the young man said.

The door opened and a young woman stood in front of them. She stared blankly at them both with no words of greeting from her mouth. Her head remained prominently uncovered. Sher Khan's facial muscles faltered into a semblance of a smile.

'*Salam Alaikum*, my daughter. You must be Noor Ali's daughter?'

'*Wa laikum Salam*, yes,' she answered. Her face didn't light up in the way his own daughters and daughters-in-law did when they faced a guest. Without a further word, she disappeared inside, leaving both standing outside. Sher Khan found this unpleasant and a novel experience to be left standing at the door. He was used to being treated with pomp and ceremony, whenever he deigned to visit any household or relatives in the village.

'Mum, there is a *buddha*, standing at the front door and talking about dad.' Sher Khan heard her distinctly say, although it was in a hushed tone. His cheeks coloured in indignation. He had never been referred to in such an offensive term as *buddha* - old man. He was always called uncle, father-figure, or the respectable term *busurgh*, but never *buddha*. The girl hadn't quite endeared herself to Sher Khan. Sher Khan, of course, made allowances that they had lived in the city for a long time and therefore they wouldn't remember him.

Then Noor Ali's wife appeared. She was pleased to see him and recognised him. She bade them to go into their *bathek*, their guest room. Sher Khan turned to the young man and thanked and tipped him for his help.

'*Bismillah*, come in, come in!' Noor Ali's wife beckoned. Sher Khan looked around at the dwelling, as he stood in the darkness of a small central courtyard. There were probably just four rooms around the central courtyard. It was a small place compared to the one they had owned in the village, which had the huge open courtyard and large *pasars*, the living rooms. He entered the *bathtek* and asked for his friend Noor Ali and was told that he had gone out shopping and would be back later.

Sher Khan sat perched on the high-back chair, unsure whether he ought to recline on the *palang*, a chaise longe. The woman, as was the Muslim custom, left him alone. It wasn't right for a woman to entertain a man, without the presence of her husband. Sher Khan looked around the room with interest.

He must have dozed off on the chair, for suddenly he heard voices. His ears pricked up as he heard his friend's voice. Through the crack between the wall and the door, he caught a glimpse of his old friend. His wife was talking to him, apparently telling him about their guest.

Sher Khan watched his friend's face with interest. He noted with dismay and humiliation that his friend's face didn't light up as he expected, at being told of his arrival. It was a bitter pill for Sher Khan to swallow. When Noor Ali walked into the room, a few seconds later, Sher Khan found it difficult to look his friend in the eye. His body worked mechanically as he got up and greeted his friend with an embrace, in the normal fashion. Sher Khan marvelled at the change in his friend, and his greeting. It didn't really tally with the glimpse of him he had caught earlier – now everything was suspect. Again he recalled that look, that naked raw look, without the urbane veneer and polish. The week of expectations of exchanging news and marvelling in each other's company seemed a dream. It was almost as if they were strangers. They exchanged news and pleasantries, yet they weren't on the same wavelength; the mutual rapport was missing.

After years and years of being worshipped as a village elder, whose every word and sigh was a law and command unto itself and whose ideas and wishes were respected, here, Sher Khan felt as if he had been robbed of his identity. It all came as a crushing blow to him. Firstly there was the attitude of the young daughter, the manner in which he had been abandoned with just a cup of tea and dried biscuits - and finally the reaction of his own friend.

His friend asked if he'd eaten. Sher Khan replied that he

wasn't hungry. Noor Ali almost shouted to his wife to find out if dinner was ready. She replied from the kitchen that it was on its way.

'Its alright, my friend. I had a heavy meal before I left the village,' Sher Khan said, trying to make light of the matter. 'Your wife didn't know I was coming.'

'You should have written. I would have gone to pick you up from the coach station.'

'I know that I should have, but it was no problem in getting to your home.'

'How long have you come for? I hope you are going to stay a week with us, at least,' his friend volunteered.

'I think that I can only spare a day,' Sher Khan heard himself saying. He didn't know what made him say that, but it just came out spontaneously. Perhaps it was due to his friend's lack of enthusiasm on hearing that he was here, or perhaps it was his pride that hadn't let him say otherwise or to tell the truth that he had indeed come to spend a week in Lahore with him, and to see the city. His friend had often stayed for weeks.

'Ah, that's a pity,' Noor Ali replied, not bothering to ask why Sher Khan could only 'spare a day', and the matter was closed.

Sher Khan dropped his gaze from his friend's. Disappointment and humiliation vied with each other in his eyes. His friend hadn't pressed him to stay. Apparently he was the unwanted guest. Sher Khan moved awkwardly on his chair.

Noor Ali kindly asked him to sit on the *palang* and put up his legs, as he must be tired from the long journey. Sher Khan did so, but as a shy awkward guest, and not as a lifelong friend. A few minutes later, mother and daughter brought in the dinner. It all fitted on one tray; there was one curry casserole, some chappatis and a small plate of salad and water. Sher Khan noted that his friend hadn't expected anything else. As he shifted the potato cubes around his plate with his chappati, Sher Khan recalled bitterly how his daughter and daughter-in-law waited hand and foot on their guests, cooking up different dishes and sweets, including those things that were not as widely available in the village as in the city, where everything was accessible round the corner, in the small bazaars. His daughter-in-law looked after their guests, even to the extent of bringing a bowl of water for him to wash his hand, and preparing a smoke pipe, a *hookah*, for him to smoke. No bowl of water had been brought for him - he was only shown the bathroom.

Next morning Sher Khan arose early and didn't know what to do with himself. Should he make it known to his hosts that he was awake? Normally, in the village, he arose with the call of the muezzin from central mosque. Here, he had heard the mosques ringing with calls at about six o'clock, but nobody had stirred in the household. Not knowing where the local mosque was, he decided to say his prayers at home, on the prayer mat provided by his host the previous night, after his ablutions.

Sitting cuddled up in his quilt on his bed, Sher Khan missed his morning *hookah*. He timed them, and the first sound he heard was at eight o'clock. Much too late! According to his village standards. Outside, the traffic was in full swing. By this time, his daughter and daughter-in-law would have finished the household chores, as well as serving breakfast. How he missed them and his early morning breakfast.

Here in Lahore, in his friend's house, he had breakfast about nine o'clock. The *parathas* and buttered hot chappatis were cooked at home, the rest of the breakfast, the halwa and the chana curry, were bought from a local breakfast take-away in the bazaar.

After some more small talk, Sher Khan decided it was time to leave. His friend and wife pressed him to stay, saying that they would show him around the bazaars and go sight-seeing to some museums and the Shalamar Gardens. Sher Khan, still doubting their sincerity, told them that he must leave. They didn't press him further. As well as the parcel of presents for his friend and his family, Sher Khan also gave money to Noor Ali's daughter. Noor Ali, in return, gave two hundred rupee notes for Sher Khan's daughter.

Sher Khan reached his next destination before eleven o'clock. He had taken a taxi from his friend's home. The hustle and bustle of the crowded scenes of the inner city ebbed away, as Sher Khan's taxi plowed through the clean, leafy, almost deserted outer suburbs of Lahore.

There were very few houses or shops. There were definitely no bazaars, but shopping plazas. He saw now only large and well-spaced-out beautiful *khoties*, villas. Sher Khan marvelled at the elegance and splendour of these beautiful buildings. At the same time, he began to feel the stirrings of unease in the pit of his stomach. The second friend, unlike Noor Ali, who lived in humble surroundings in the inner city, had certainly progressed well in the world. Sher Khan had heard how well his friend had done. How he had opened a factory with the help of his three sons, since he had left the village – he had, however, not expected this.

The reality of the gulf between his own standard of living and the way of life of his second friend washed over him. As he paid the driver, he stood outside the gigantic and elegant villa of his friend. The taxi disappeared and he found himself standing outside the white filigree wrought-iron gate. There wasn't a soul in the wide street to be seen.

Sher Khan peered through the large gates and saw a beautifully kept green lawn, bordered with neat flower beds, and the elegant alabaster pillars of the large porch with its marble chipped floor. He tried to open the gates, but they wouldn't open. He shook them hard, but to no avail. Suddenly a large dog bounded out from somewhere at the back of the villa. It stopped on the other side of the gates and bared its teeth at Sher Khan, who stepped back in fear, his heart beginning to thud in his chest. A middle-aged man appeared and stood behind the dog. From his clothing and general demeanour, Sher Khan guessed this man to be one of his friend's home helpers or servants.

'*Assalama-Alaikum, Aba Jee*. Did you want to see anybody?'

'Yes. I have come to see my friend Mohammed. Does he live here?'

'Yes. He has gone to the factory, but he will be here soon. I'll take the dog away first and I'll open the gates so that you can come inside and wait for *Sahib*. You should have rung the bell. It is over there on the pillar.'

'Oh, I didn't see it,' said Sher Khan, looking around the gates.

'Just wait there while I press the button to open the gates, you see, they are electronically controlled.'

Sher Khan stood and watched, marvelling as the gates parted as if by magic. They disappeared behind the high walls, draped with shrubs and rose bushes.

It was at that very moment that a shining, well-polished black saloon drew up to the villa and, finding the gates open, just went through. Sher Khan moved aside and looked carefully into the car. He saw his friend Mohammed sitting in the front seat beside one of his sons. Mohammed stared back at him blankly to Sher Khan's dismay. There was no trace of recognition in that look, or if there was, it was well hidden. It was almost as if Mohammed had looked right through a wall and not at a lifelong friend, whom he had seen only three years ago in the village and had grown up with.

The car disappeared from sight as it went round the back of the villa. Sher Khan remained standing outside, his mind and heart in a whirl.

The manservant returned.

'*Baba Jee*, Mohammed *Sahib* have returned. I'll inform them about you.' Sher Khan noted the plural use of 'have' and 'them' when the servant referred to his employer.

Sher Khan tried to swim out of the swamp of humiliation and claw back some of his own dignity and respect.

'No, it's okay. Just give him this.' He passed the second parcel he had brought with him to the manservant.

'Who shall I say gave this?'

'It doesn't matter. Say an old friend from his other life. He probably doesn't remember me. I'll be off then. *Assalam Alaikum.*'

'*Walaikum Salam.* Are you sure you won't come in? Shall I call a taxi for you?'

'No, it's alright, I'll find one on the way.' Sher Khan didn't want to bump into his friend and therefore hastened away.

It was easier said than done, Sher Khan thought, as he walked forlornly from street to street, hoping to catch a glimpse of a taxi. In this area people had cars. They didn't need taxis, he told himself, as he went into one *khotie* to ask if someone would call a taxi for him. In the end, one kind young man drove him to Lahore's coach station, where he caught the coach back to his village.

Mohammed was handed the parcel that Sher Khan had brought for him. He looked at the gauche parcel with distaste. He wanted to distance himself from his past life in the village.

'An old friend of yours came and left this, but he wouldn't come to meet you.'

'Yes, yes, I understand,' Mohammed replied hastily. He recalled the old man and the face, but didn't want to be reminded of it. 'Here, you take it Ali. It is probably some *sag*, some spinach. I've had my fill of it, in all those years I spent in that village.'

The servant took the parcel, but he was disconcerted at his master's manner and words. He recalled the look on the old man's face, as the latter stumbled away after seeing the black car. He carried it to his quarters, at the back of the villa, and gave it to his wife. She marvelled at the parcel's contents as she unwrapped it. As well as fresh vegetables, there was a tin of ghee, purified butter, home-made pastries and three hand-embroidered pillow cases, with crocheted edges.

At that moment, Sher Khan was deep in thought, in the coach, wrestling and debating with himself as to what plausible excuse he could give to his family and fellow villagers for returning after just one day, when he was supposed to be away for two weeks.

The only plausible reason he could come up with was that the city wasn't for him, nor its people, the *sheries*.

Jamie

Christopher B. Skyrme

It happened again that day. One minute everything felt right and then, again, that stomach-wrenching feeling. As if I had suddenly been turned upside-down. As if my legs had been violently kicked from under me. At the door he had paused, turned round, looked at me and then come rushing back to hug me. And then he was gone. Through the window I watched him disappear from sight and, as he went, my dreams, my hopes, my soul vanished with him.

It had been another ordinary day, although that morning had been slightly more difficult than usual. My fault entirely – but then you sometimes just have to leave the ironed-shirt order of your established routine and enter the exciting, dangerous world, if only to feel that for once you belong. Anyway, that morning, when the alarm rang at six-thirty, it took me several minutes just to force my dance-aching limbs into action. And then the car wouldn't start. 'Of all the bloody mornings!' I yelled into the empty street. I tucked my case under my arm and headed for the bus-stop.

It took ages to get to school. I arrived bleary eyed and bus-traumatised. I sat huddled in the staff-room, coaxing the black coffee into my bloodstream. I was desperate for a cigarette, but since the ban by the 'concerned' collective, the only place to go for a smoke was outside on the pavement and the way I was feeling I just knew I couldn't manage even that simple journey.

The morning passed in a routine kind of fashion. Helen, who I was teaching with, had distributed gaily coloured paper and garish, gooey paint to each table. The class spent a remarkably concentrated hour drawing their own faces. I remember saying to Helen that we ought to organise an eye inspection for the class – such were their vivid imaginations. Fascinating how, even equipped with the specially non-breakable mirrors, they still saw faces that were entirely unlike their own!

We hung the finished self-portraits to dry around the room and ended the morning with a story in the Reading Corner. Helen and I were happy with the sticky results of the morning's work.

After lunch, Ros called me over in the staff room. One of the helpers in Reception was ill and she wanted me to take over for her. I smiled across and said, 'of course'. I wish I hadn't.

Ros explained to me, after the inevitable communal song with actions, that I was to take one of the 'problem' kids aside and coach him in maths and reading skills. Fighting the urge to shout 'special needs', I nodded agreement and moved over to one of the tiny blue chairs by the window.

It was then that I was first introduced to Jamie. Scruffy, wearing faded blue hand-me-down jeans and a food-bespeckled T-shirt, his pale blonde hair sticking up in all directions, he looked just like any other kid in the school. He sat down on one of the chairs next to me and I introduced myself. We started working on some simple maths exercises. Jamie had a photocopied sheet of circles and squares, which he had to colour in. Sitting watching him, I couldn't help noticing his enthusiasm for the task. His tongue poked out from the corner of his mouth, his forehead was creased with concentration. Gripping the coloured pen as though his life depended on it, he laboriously copied out his work – getting it hopelessly wrong, but managing to create a far more interesting pattern than that on the master copy.

After a time we abandoned this exercise and I asked him if he'd like to choose a book from the Reading Corner. His face lit up with an intensity of dazzling brightness and he raced across the classroom, returning with a well-worn book clasped in his hand. I don't remember the title of the book, but it was set in a forest and told the story of a rabbit thug who raced around the wood on his yellow scooter, beating up all the other creatures.

Jamie adored this book. It was apparent from the outset that he couldn't read, but he almost knew the text by heart. As I read each page, his lips moved in synch to my voice. His face shone as he pored over the colourful pictures, pointing out tiny details. When we got to the part where the rabbit started hitting the other animals, he became serious and concerned. Before each page could be turned he would stop, look at me and then look back to the page, leaning over and kissing the animal better, intoning in a sing-song voice, 'poor little hedgehog' or 'poor little caterpillar' or whatever the injured creature might be. There was something profoundly moving in that gesture.

That afternoon seemed to race past and it only seemed five minutes before it was home time. As I watched Jamie cross the playground on his way home, I felt that churning sensation that has become so familiar. 'He's just another kid,' I told myself, as I walked across to put away the coloured pens.

The next day, during lunch break, I was on duty in the junior playground. I love that time. Standing in the middle of a sea of screaming kids, a blur of colours running in all directions, laughter never very far away. I was sorting out a minor dispute over a football when I suddenly felt a tiny hand thrust into mine. I looked down and there was Jamie. He tugged at my arm.

'Are you going to read me my story today?' I wanted to laugh, but the desperate look on his face silenced me. Gently I led him back to his own playground, explaining that he was too small to come on the juniors' space and that he shouldn't wander about the school. I felt a fraud. Feeling that little hand in mine, I'd felt touched that he'd sought me out. Secretly I hoped that he'd do it again.

Over coffee in the staff room, I mentioned the incident to Helen. She laughed and said that being a gay man and so gentle with the kids was a positive influence on them, and not to worry. But something in her tone held a note of concern. I pressed the matter further and Helen told me about Jamie's sister. I recognised the girl immediately from the description. Always on her own, she was a peculiar child. She had a face of amazing whiteness, so pale she was almost translucent. She appeared to have no friends and, when in a large group, would self-consciously scratch at her arms or legs until they bled. Alarm bells were beginning to sound in my head.

Over the next few weeks I tried to distance myself from

Jamie. But each time that little hand slipped into mine, I silently cried with happiness. I began to depend on these incidents. To look forward with anticipation to his request, 'Are you going to read me my story today?'

Then, one Friday afternoon, it happened. I was in the junior class, tidying up after a particularly hectic plasticene modelling session, as the kids started to drift home. I was bending down, trying to scrape a nasty plasticene mess off the floor, when a blur of pale blue rushed across the room and flung itself into my arms. It was Jamie. He threw both arms around me and, clinging to me, kissed me gently on the neck. I didn't know what to do. And, as I crouched there wondering how to prise him off, I felt a shadow move across me. I looked up straight into the eyes of Jamie's father. The eyes were bloodshot, their whites a tarnished yellow colour. I'd seen that look before. A few years before I'd been in Paris with a boyfriend. Late at night, we were sat outside Notre Dame, drinking cheap beer out of a bottle and debating where to go next, when a man had appeared. Within seconds he had assessed the situation. Two gay men, two pissed gay men. Easy prey. I remember his cold piercing eyes as he drew a knife out of his pocket, muttering, 'Pédés. Pédés. Sales Pédés.' Jamie's father didn't have to say anything. That look was eloquent in its hate and anger. I stood up slowly, gently pushing Jamie away from me and murmured something banal about his story...

One minute everything had felt right and then, again, that stomach-wrenching feeling. As if my legs had been violently kicked from under me. At the door Jamie had paused, turned, looked at me, and then come rushing back to hug me. And then he was gone.

Legoland on Mescalin

Catriona Smith

'And the rest, luv.' Breath blasted my face with l'air du Special Brew.

'There isn't any more. I was only off to the shop,' I squeaked indignantly.

In the dim stairwell light, his baseball cap rendered his face shadowed, impenetrable. He tucked the money inside his bomber jacket, above the threatening bulge in his breast pocket. He frisked me, flinching as his hands crossed my chest. In embarrassment?

'Aye well, luv. You'd best get off home then.' Like a ticket collector, apologetic after an argument over a Saver Return. No more then? No opportunistic grope against the piss-stinking, graffitied wall? He stepped back, releasing me, sauntering away with a stiff nonchalance, like a man disturbed during a slash.

I pelted up the stairs. Along the landing. Key. Door stabbed. Living room stormed into.

'That,' I said, addressing the wall (yes, the wall), 'that was not bloody funny. I go out for one, just one, bar of Galaxy and a pint of milk. End stairwell, bottom flight, and I'm relieved of my dosh by one of Major's more enterprising millions! Not funny.'

'Not funny, sweetie?' When concrete speaks, it purrs seductively. 'You little tease. Parading about with...'

'About £2.59 actually,' I snapped.

'Darling,' she oozed, smooth and harmless as a smoking river of lava, 'violence is soo sexy. Aggression has always been sexy. People come here and see...'

'Legoland on mescalin?'

'Exactly.' A voice so silky ought to be pouring me a martini and massaging my feet. 'The sheer brutality of soaring concrete cliffs and cavernous, urinous stairwells breeds an itchy, lusty frustration. If Kim Basinger bound and Isabella Rosellini beaten get them groping all over the

Odeon, then my little adventure playground gets them steamed up, no trouble. But I'm a pussycat, really. An urban pussycat.'

'So concrete's sexy cos it's *brutal?*'

'Most people are ashamed, so they mask it with dread, or condescension, or letters to the Manchester Evening News. The rest come and live here. Hornily ever after.'

I flopped on the sofa. 'Salford Quays?' I raised my eyebrows.

'Full on strip show. All that glass – leaves nothing to the imagination. Too southern. Too Essex. Nah. Give 'em a sniff of glass and lots of concrete so they can eulogise about their northern roots, and you get...'

'Yeah yeah. Manchester's answer to Paris's Left Bank. Yawn.' Moving to the kitchen. Sink. Kettle. Hob. Matches. 'Anyway, you haven't answered my question.' I hovered in the doorway. 'Why me? Why today?'

The wall sighed. The Indian print bedspread hanging on it flapped as if in an apologetic shrug.

'I'm sorry, luv.' Huh. About time. 'It wasn't for you. It was for him downstairs. He...'

'You mean you set him up, then? You?'

'Of course, sweetie.' I swear if plasterboard could smile toothily... 'Nothing ever just happens, here.'

Oh no, nothing ever just happens here. I learnt that at the beginning of our, er, friendship. You get mugged on the walkway? It's your own greed come to get you in a black balaclava. Becoming a bit of a couch potato recently? You'll soon have a visitor through the window at 3 a.m. to, er, tax your telly. And no, they're not real live dealers down there by the offy, they're just little guardians of enterprise culture, grown a size too big for its Reeboks. See those three cars burnt out on the playing fields? One way to solve the energy crisis, innit?

So I talk to my living room wall, right? You got a problem with that, eh? It talks back, an' all. Does too! Well, I talk to the wall but the whole estate answers. When concrete speaks, it's not to just anybody. It's Hulme, it's got a personality, see? After twenty years of being celebrated and lambasted and photographed. Twenty years of twentysomethings banging their creative craniums on the walls, it's kind of soaked it all up. It's got a mind of it's own, it can talk.

Eh? 'Course rock can think! That's what electronics is based on, silicon chips. 'Course rock can talk! That's what geology's all about, innit? So why not concrete, eh? So pull up a chair, 'cos Hulme, urban sexpot and civic blackspot, has a story to tell you.

When I found out Hulme was alive, I was in the kind of foul mood that if I was a town planner, the Arndale would seem like suitable revenge. My fella was out the door with his sweet ego deflating faster than the price of shares in Factory records. I'd been to the bottle bank, for a bit of therapeutic smashing, and six month's Liebfraumilch consumption was now aquarium gravel. And those Guatemalan ethnic cushions, they were fairly quivering every time I came near the sofa, such a thumping I'd given them. I slid gently over to the wall. Slammed my fist against it. Experimentally, like. Well, how was I to know?

'You can stop that right now!' The voice was authoritarian, nannyish. Check left shoulder. Right. Nope. Just me in the flat. What the..?

'I said, you can stop right now. You needn't take it out on me. I'm not impressed, you know. I've seen it all before.' Jeez, Mary Poppins in my very own living room. If walls had midriffs, this one would creek with whalebone.

'All you nice, white, middle class girls, on the run from your backgrounds. Privileged backgrounds.' I opened my mouth. 'You come and play housey amongst the proles,' a snigger, 'and dress up as urban warriors,' snort, 'and think that you're living out some kind of Naked Lunch ideal. Year after year!'

'Now wait a minute...'

'Where does that leave me, eh? Just the Hovis of a Naked Lunchburger?'

'Now hold on.' Alright, I was talking to the wall! Bear with me. 'Wait a minute. We're not all,' I sneered, 'from *Surrey*. We're not all,' I spat, 'from *public school*. I don't have a dog, piece of string or otherwise! Some of us have got something to run from...'

Like any good nanny, she babied me good and proper. She looks after her chicks, does Hulme. Shelters them until they learn to fly on their own. Seen enough heads banging against this wall and enough nails scratching it down. Jeez, so many screwed up kids (white, middle class or otherwise) seek sanctuary here, when they knock it down it won't just be good old deportation-dodger Viraj Mendis who needs a monument. But like everything else, she picked me out for a purpose. Oh yes.

'You all come here, do your bit of self expression, then you all toddle off to live out some rural idyll in Wales. Well, what about me?' Injured sniff. 'Oh sure,' snort, 'you write a few songs, you take a few photos, but what do I get? Still held up as a worse excess of the Sixties than,' spat with venom, '*purple loon pants*! If I had a penny for every time...'

How do you placate several thousand tons of concrete? Hesitantly, I guess.

'Well, um, er, I'm sure people appreciate you, erm, Hulme. Can I call you Hulme?' Do I take that slight ripple in the plasterboard as a nod? 'Well, erm, people tell me all the time what an, ah, stimulating place it is, sorry, you are to live. What about the Hulme Festival? And Hulme Community Arts? For such a young, er, estate you've come a long way...'

'Always the cocoon and never the butterfly!' she sighed. 'Well, I'm going to get my chance. And you're going to help me. I'm sick of being the dream estate that never wakes up. I've always wanted to... No, you'll laugh.'

'I won't, I promise. On my tie-dye bedspread.'

'They're going to, going to knock me down.' I nodded. That I knew. 'They want, they want to make me into office blocks! You've got to help me!' When doomed concrete begs, who can resist? Is a heart of stone enough?

* * *

'...Don't see why not.' Tina slurped her tea in the hazy sunshine. 'Don't see why not. Loads of stories about spirit of the forest, you know, Pan and that. People are always talking about Hulme 'aving character. Don't see why, if some ancient forest can be alive, this pile of concrete can't be an' all. No offence meant, like,' she added, kicking the door jamb affectionately with her para boot. 'What's it got to do with you, anyway? What 'ave you got yourself tied up in, mate?'

It was the next afternoon, and I was round Tina's drinking tea and watching the casual, half hearted dealing going on in the square below.

'Oh you know, nothing.' Liar, liar. Pants on fire. 'Oh look. What do you reckon on the guy in the blue jacket?'

'Buying,' she said confidently. 'Can see the whites of his eyes. Waiting for him in number twenty-seven.' A shrewd, assessing glance. 'Nah. I know when you're up to something, Morrison, and I ain't never seen a cat look more like it's got the cream. What gives?'

'Sorry, Tina, no can do right now.' I looked down, scuffed the floorboards with the toe of my boot. The boards appeared to writhe in delight like a hound having its belly rubbed. 'Teen, can I ask you something?' Spit it out kid, the floorboards creaked. 'What, er, what made you first move in here?'

'Oh you know. Cheap. Me mates around. Loads of other people like me.' She chewed on the end of a dreadlock, thoughtfully. 'But you know sumfink? I fit in here. I belong. I dunno. I guess I feel I've got some reason for being here, somehow.' She smiled a tight embarrassed smile, began picking at her chipped black nail varnish.

I could feel a gleeful buzz in the wall behind me.

'Oh, you have, you little feline beauty,' a voice whispered, like the rustle of wind in smog-ridden treetops, 'and she most certainly has...'

* * *

'Oh darling.' My mother turned away from the window a little too abruptly. 'It's so wonderfully... colourful, so, so full of character. I do like your window. The boards are so... olde worlde. Like shutters, are they? Oh I see.' A short, baffled pause. 'Gosh, aren't people here friendly? So considerate! That man down there said hello to me three times as I was getting out of the car and he asked if there was anything I wanted. Well, I said a coat of paint round here wouldn't go amiss.' I cringed at her brittle laughter. 'And look, people keep driving up to chat to him all the time! Is he a friend of yours, sweetheart? No?'

This was going to be a long slog. Best open the fondant fancies now. Keep her scoffing. Keep her distracted...

'Alison, darling,' her smile was so strained it would have an osteopath fairly cracking his own knuckles with glee, 'isn't it just a little... urban?'

Yeah. A little urban that won't grow up into a suburban.

'Oh Mum, I like it, it's got...' No, I won't say it, I promise I won't. 'It's got, erm, brilliant views.'

'Alison, sweetheart.' Change of tone. Grinding. Like my mother's gear changes. 'Your father and I, well, we really would feel so much better if we knew you weren't always struggling financially.' (Translation: When are you going to get a proper job? Like one with a wage, for instance). The scrape of nylon marked her ample thighs crossing. 'Darling, we would like to see you doing a job in which you're happy.' (But don't you think you've pandered to your social conscience long enough?). 'In fact, I, I hope you don't think I'm being Mrs Bossy Mother, but I brought you some leaflets. You've got such a head for figures.' Must get it from my dad eh? Along with a few scars and bruises that stubbornly refuse to fade. 'Seems a pity to see it all wasted. So I've brought you a few leaflets.' (Application forms?) 'Just in case you...' Injured sniff.

'Oh, that's really very kind of you, Mum.' No sniggering at the back there, wall. You're not the only one who doesn't want to grow up to be an office block. 'Lovely.' See? My smile was so strained I could almost hear it twanging. Hey, Hulme, with any luck I'll be supporting myself before long, eh? 'Hey, there's some carrot cake in the kitchen. Shall we...?'

* * *

So, a few weeks had passed and you see, Hulme had a little scheme for me, a role to play. The night in question came and I didn't want to do it. I tried to bunk off. Stomped round the walkways. Stood on the top landing of my favourite Crescent, John Nash, squashed and comfortable like a lived-in sofa. A metaphorical foot tapped. When concrete waits, it waits patiently. Attrition wears people away as surely as it does rock.

'Alright, alright. Don't pout your walkway at me like that. I'll do it. But don't be surprised if you get City Challenged into being the new Canary Wharf and I end up wearing a Next suit and being groped behind the filing cabinets. I'll do it!'

Ever fallen asleep on an Intercity train? Been jerked awake at a station and jumped out thinking it's Piccadilly? Then found out that you're marooned in Newton-le-Willows on a rain-drizzled November night? Went to bed. Drifted off. Found myself derailed from dreaming in the same way...

A huge, cavernous room. I was on a flat plain next to what appeared to be a tree trunk-sized Parker Pen. Voices booming far above me in diesel-fumed air. A meeting? That's what I was told to expect...

'What's wrong with being a suburb?' the one nearest to me boomed on my left. 'Get yourself a few semis, bit of stone cladding, a Tesco's, drop your insurance premium and you're laughing. What about a snappier name, say East Trafford?'

'But what about the existing community?' A worried, social worker kind of voice, further behind me than the first. You could almost catch the rustle of corduroy trousers on the scale of an entire postal district.

'Them that'll wise up will stay. Them that won't, I'm sure we can find them some quiet estate out of sight of the Olympic Bid office, eh, Wythenshawe?' A murmur from the south end. I whirled, but all that was visible from that corner was... an oversized marquee? No, well, are you sure about this? A huge pair of trainers?

'And I'm sure the rest'll hitch up their dogs to disused ambulances and go find some rural landowner to hassle.'

'Yes, thank you Trafford, I'm sure we've all taken that on board.' Hasty, stuttering, a clipped voice bang in front of me. The vague outline of a collar and tie, the height of a four-storey building. The chair of this bizarre parliament of the city? 'But we must take Chorlton's suggestion seriously. Is provision being made for the part of Hulme that can't, or won't, become the new Salford Quays? Wythenshawe? Can you take them?' A twitch of the gargantuan left foot. 'Well, I suppose we have to take that as a yes. Gentlemen? Shall we move to a vote?'

'Wait a minute,' I squeaked in the darkness. Unseen gazes shifted, seeming as slow as continents drifting together. 'Wait a minute. You didn't ask Hulme to this meeting.'

'Good gracious! What the..? Where?' Hastily whispered conferral. 'My dear young, er, lady,' a voice drawled behind me. Didsbury, judging by the flash of horn-rimmed glasses. 'Hulme is... how can I put it, in animate terms? Hulme is but a little girl flitting between the dressing-up box and her sister's make up drawer. She refuses to grow up. She refuses to take her role seriously. She snarls in the face of any suggestion we come up with. So we have to take the decision for her, as her, ahem, companions and neighbours. Hulme will be a business park.'

'She's told me what she wants. It's perfectly feasible. It's got everything there – tourist revenue, nice backhander from the National Trust, gushing praise from the planning department.' Got to keep talking, got to keep talking, can't stop or they might cut me off before the first phrase drifts into their leviathan brains. 'You'll be media darlings for the next twenty years! The South Bank Show will be under your duvet before you can say *urban regeneration...*'

'Please, do elucidate.' Chorlton wafted eagerness, like a teacher who has just spotted a listening pupil in the middle of his expansion of the finer points of Macbeth. Deep breath. Huge, slow consciousnesses need it socked to them gently.

'Well. Hulme wants to grow up. She wants to grow up into a forest.' A few stirrings, a few snorts, gentle as smoke from a cooling tower, but I felt the weight of their attention. 'Let the urban jungle flower into a real jungle. Hulme wants to keep all the, er, humans who live there, but she wants to give them a bigger and better adventure playground, wood not concrete. And nobody at the Town Hall need ever see anything but trees and flowers and tourist revenue...'

'Well, a civic park perhaps.' Didsbury's measured, elderly professor tones appeared to mull it over. 'Even a city farm, but a forest! Preposterous. We could never allow it. Think of the...' The voices receded. I felt warm breath rushing past my ears. A last ditch persuasion...

'An urban theme park! Historic reconstructions! If you won't allow it, she'll do it by herself!' I yelled into the howling gale. 'Look! She's got everything she needs...'

I was hurtling back to waking again, flying through the air. Twigs whipped at me. Dogs barked, and a voice close to my ear whispering, 'Oh yes my pretty, we done good...' Princess Parkway roared below me like a river, and I thought I could see... the Crescents stirring? Nah! But, like four enormous reptiles, dragons, maybe? Waking as if from a twenty year sleep! Yawning and stretching and flicking their tails in each other's faces and bickering about who's going to get a maiden for breakfast! Nah, I'm dreaming still, remember? Aren't I?

Alighting on the platform of my bed. No, won't open my eyes yet. Need a rest, don't I? Put myself through all that for you, eh? Don't even know if it's worked, either. The silence had an overbearingly smug quality. I reached out my hand to the wall. Eyes still closed. Check the birds singing. Check the sun shining on my closed lids, check the... Stretch. Yawn. Patted the wall reassuringly. Hey baby, I'm here. I ain't done gone an' leftcha...

Rough. Channelled. Warm to the touch. Not concrete. Bark?

'Oh Lordy.' I leapt out of bed, leaves crackling underfoot. 'You, you jammy little urban urchin, you. You little..! You've gone and..!'

Words couldn't do it justice. A walk might.

Taking a walk that morning, seeing the changes. Yes, I suppose nuts and berries is a diet you can get used to. The Crescents were all snuggled up together again, a nest of reptilian contentment, a faded army parka dangling from John Nash's jaws. Quite a few odd-shaped outcrops of rock round here, aren't there? All huddled together and just about the height of a six storey block... Can just about see the roof of G-Mex, rising like some ancient burial mound the far side of the river... Stumbled across a wildcat just now. Rabbit in its jaws and a smile as smug as me mate Tina's... Best see about breakfast, eh? I shouldered my crossbow and strode down towards the clearing.

'You know, Hulme, I'd shake you by the hand if I thought you had one anywhere amongst the undergrowth. You snazzy little planning blunder, you. Now, where'd Tina hook that rabbit...?'

As I passed the bloke propped up against the oak tree, he called out to me.

'Not seen Will Scarlet anywhere around, 'ave yer? Little swine, still not seen to that loose shoe on my mare yet.' I shrugged. His face looked familiar.

'Oi.' He reached inside his leather jerkin. 'Wench. Here's that two crowns and fifty nine pennies I owe you.'

Queens' Court

José Gent

Rose picked her way along the dark, cobbled side street, avoiding oily puddles and piles of refuse. A woman came up from the basement kitchen of a restaurant to throw a bin bag onto the heap by the door and Rose shrank back out of sight against the wall. Last week the woman had shouted abuse in a strange language Rose didn't understand and once a man had thrown a lighted cigarette stub at her from the same doorway, laughing spitefully. The pavement there overflowed with bags and cartons. Later on, towards midnight, a van would come, looking for Liz.

'It's getting late, I wonder where she is,' thought Rose. 'I haven't seen her anywhere round town since last week. Maybe she took that flat the people from the van found for her, although she told me she wouldn't. She's a fool. If I had the chance of my own warm pad, I'd move in right away, and I wouldn't let anyone scare me out of it.'

Warm air blew round her feet from the extractor fan of the kitchen below, reeking of fried prawns and stale fat. Liz slept there, next to the vent, her head resting on her overturned shopping trolley, more often than not with nothing else between her and the cold stones, the draught from the fan ruffling the hem of her skirt against the pavement.

'I don't know how she can bear to spend night after night in this stinking atmosphere,' Rose thought, 'however warm it is. The fan goes off at four o'clock anyway and it's perishing cold by then.'

The woman disappeared down the narrow stairway and Rose continued on her way towards the brightly lit main street. It was too early for the van and the people who brought it only stayed for a few minutes. When Liz was awake, they gave her drinks and a blanket to replace the one they had brought the night before, knowing she would have lost that one. If she was asleep, they didn't disturb her, they just laid the blanket over her, very gently, and went on their way.

Rose reached the corner. A massive, richly carved and gilded wooden arch towered across the way, its fierce, red lacquered dragons guarding the Chinese quarter of the city. A few couples hurried towards the car park, huddled into their coats, heads bent against the wind, feeling the cold after the warmth of the restaurant they had just left. On the opposite corner, her short leather jacket worn open over a thin, low-cut T-shirt, her brief mini-skirt revealing long, lovely legs, a girl stood motionless, oblivious of the cold, her face without expression.

The Vice Squad were out in force, cruising round and round the block in their big white vans, but they ignored the silent girl. They were after the dealers and the minders, the men who controlled the girl and others like her. Rose had nothing to do with them. She had learned to be wary, keep herself to herself. It was better that way. She'd been let down by false friends too often. These days she relied on no one, not even Liz.

Sirens wailed in the distance, echoing between the high walls of dignified, deserted office buildings, their impressive front doors closed, their only occupants the security guards. Sometimes, emerging from the loading bay into the back alley, the men would stop to chat, but they never managed to entice her into their warm rooms, where they whiled away the long nights of duty brewing cups of tea.

There was Liz, half way along the main street, enthroned on the steps outside Li Lin's restaurant. Floodlit in the glow from the magnificent Chinese Arch across the way, a dumpy, rotund Elizabeth Regina serenely acknowledged the tributes bestowed on her by the patrons leaving Li Lin's, her pockets full of coins and five pound notes. She would be waiting for her courtiers to arrive in the small blue van, bringing her a new velvet cloak along with the banquet. Liz had a vivid imagination.

'Silly old Liz,' thought Rose. 'Who does she think she is, holding court out there in the main street? No wonder she gets robbed so often, carrying all that money around with her. She'll never learn. It's about time she settled down for the night, before it gets any colder.'

Rose shivered. There would be snow on the hills tonight, and, though it hardly ever snowed in the city, the wind was bitter, snatching greedily at the fallen leaves in the car park, swirling them around with scraps of paper, rolling empty cans noisily along the gutter, playing a wild, untidy game. She wished Liz would leave her pitch and settle down. She would stay with her tonight, they could keep warm together. They could spread out those cartons she'd seen outside the kitchen door and lie on them, sharing the blanket. If Liz didn't hurry, someone else would take them. Then she would have to lie on the stone pavement and that would do her arthritis no good at all.

Another siren wailed, closer now, and suddenly one end of the street was blocked by two white vans. The tall, slim girl across the way melted out of sight into the shadows and Rose pressed herself against the wall, as a speeding car swerved past her and screeched to a halt in front of the police vans, with another in hot pursuit. It was the second car that skidded into the steps outside Li Lin's, toppling over at a crazy angle onto the Royal Throne, its blue light still flashing in the few seconds of eerie silence that followed the clash of metal against stone.

She didn't wait to look. There was no need. Rose turned and fled before the police helicopter's beam of bright, white light could slice through the soft, golden glow of the street lights and trap her there, trembling with shock, racked with guilt. It was her fault. She should have gone down the street to Liz, risked her sudden temper, persuaded her to leave her throne and settle down early for the night in the side street, warm for a few hours, however foul the smell from the vent in the wall.

The van would be along soon with soft voices calling Liz, bringing the blanket, cups of soup and tea. By then the Ambulance would have gone, yet another siren wailing, lamenting the passing of a queen and, not finding Liz, they would move away, leaving Rose to her memories and dreams. Beautiful, shy Rosita, whose brilliant, wide green eyes had once bewitched everyone who knew her in her prime.

'Rosita, my queen, my ravishing Rosita,' the old man used to say. 'I could buy you all the emeralds in the world and still find none to match your glorious eyes.'

Life was good then, sheltered and secure, but she had no claim on his mansion when he died. He had no family and his friends, who once had fawned on her and curried her favours to flatter him, had no time for her now. The gracious old house in the leafy suburb was sold by his solicitors for development and, broken hearted, she was left to fend for herself.

Out of the wind in the safe, concealing darkness of the side street, she crouched between the bin bags, trembling still, and desolate, aware that she must forget yet another friend she would never see again, so cold that she knew she would not sleep. The people in the van were very kind, but it never occurred to them to leave a blanket for a cat.

Watching Wanting

Glenda Brassington

It was on a night like this that I would see him standing in his room, across the patchwork of lawns and vegetable plots that separate our buildings. He was there every night, all night, always standing. Sometimes he would have his back to the window and occasionally I would see him walking forwards and backwards, disappearing and then reappearing, like the little figures in a clock that pop out on the hour. The clock in the city centre has Lady Godiva appearing on a white horse while Peeping Tom is peeping at her from a window above. I decided to call him Tom. When I first saw him I thought he was watching me. I would try and keep out of his sight. Then I got quite used to him being there at that safe distance and I found that I liked it, I liked the fact that someone was so obsessed with me that they would stand there for hours just to watch me. After watching him, though, I realised that he hadn't even noticed me. He never looked in my direction, he didn't seem to be standing there for any reason. By ten o'clock he was always gone.

I remember one Friday night he went at quarter to ten. I carried on sitting by the window in case he reappeared. The baby downstairs started crying again. It never stops crying, but then neither does the mother. The two of them still share the room below mine. Most people only stay here a short time, while they're waiting for a council flat or trying to save a deposit. There are seven of us altogether in this one house. Seven 'studio flats', as the advert said. Each flat consisting of one room, with a shower in one corner and a cooker in the other. It's funny to think that at one time this house would have been occupied by just one family, and their maid I suppose. Actually, there's a family that live next door. A family and an au-pair. Mr Webster has been here longer than me, he's got a room on the top floor. I've only ever seen him a handful of times in the eight years that I've lived here. I think he tries to hide from people. I've noticed him hovering on the landing above as I've been coming in, waiting for me to go inside my room before he'll descend. I'll shout up hello, just to let him know I'm aware of what he's doing. I'm not sure how old he is, but he's definitely retired. Gary, who lives above me, reckons that all Mr Webster has got in his room is a sleeping bag, a lamp and his clothes, and he's in there most nights. He's always out during the day. I'm not sure where he goes but I've seen him reading in the library a couple of times. I don't know what he's doing living in a place like this. I was thinking of moving out at one time but I've got used to it now. It's familiar and comfortable at least. Tom didn't seem to be coming back.

I picked up the paper to see what was on television. A picture of a young black lad grinning at the camera caught my eye. Beneath was the heading, 'Twelve Year Old Stabbed to Death in Racist Attack.' It's only the free paper, I won't pay to read such horrible stories. Only, they're not stories, are they? They're truths, horrible truths. I got up to check that the door was locked. I know it sounds funny, but I felt quite safe when he was there, when I could see his figure across the way. Terry Wogan was muttering away quietly to himself in the corner. I always leave the television on for company, besides, I don't like it when it is quiet, I start hearing things.

I watched the woman in the house next to Tom fold up her washing whilst a young boy sat on the kitchen table, in his pyjamas, swinging his legs to and fro. They looked so cosy in their little square of light in the middle of the dark night. They looked so cosy and safe. I wanted to be that young boy.

I hate this time of year, with its long dark nights. It's hard to believe that in the summer I could be sitting outside a pub at this time, enjoying the last of the sunset. It feels like something people do in other countries, that I can remember doing once in a blurred vision, maybe on holiday. The summers always become overshadowed by winter's long overcoat. Mind you, I could see him better in the winter as he never drew the curtains when he put the light on. His window is a rectangle on its side, so it was like Cinescope. Sometimes I think I would forget that he was a real person, except he wasn't that real to me, only his figure was real and that was incomplete, as the window ledge came up to his upper thighs. I never saw his legs.

People always ask me how I can live on my own. It's a nice room, big enough for two. I used to imagine Tom sitting in my red velvet chair, resting a cup of tea on the arm, whilst laughing at Blind Date. They tell me I should get a dog. I've never wanted a pet though, as they die. A woman where I used to work took two weeks off when her dog died. When her husband had died the year before, she'd taken one day off for the funeral. Besides, it's not fair to keep a pet in one room on a first floor. It's alright for humans though. I might feel safer with a dog. We were broken into five times that year. They only got into my room once and they took my television; there's nothing else for them to take. It had only cost me twenty pounds two years before. It was black and white but I'd painted coloured flowers all over the brown sides, so I called it my colour television. I managed to get a new one from Gary upstairs. He sold me his for fifty pounds, as he'd just been made redundant and needed the money. This one really was colour. Terry Wogan looked like he'd just been to the Caribbean and contracted jaundice. He was sort of a cross between bright orange and fluorescent yellow. It was nice just to watch the changing patterns of colour. It reminded me of looking through a small kaleidoscope I had when I was young.

I remember watching Tom one night at his window and, for some reason, he was all dressed up in a white shirt instead of his usual dark T-shirts. His hair was slicked back in its carefree way and it flopped in front of his eyes as he lit a cigarette, then left it dangling from his lips, the smoke drifting up in front of his face. He looked like an old forties film star or maybe even something from a Levi's advert. He stood there just looking down, then as he took the cigarette from his lips, he turned and looked at me. I mean, he was too far away to properly see his eyes but I could tell he was staring at me. His gaze was fixed on mine and neither of us moved. I felt myself burning with embarrassment but I couldn't turn away. My head was throbbing and felt full of noise. I stood there, hardly breathing, while he finished his cigarette. He threw the fag-end out of the window and turned away out of sight. I wanted to scream and laugh and cry all at once. He had finally let me into his life.

After this, I knew that he felt the same way about me but that he was too shy or too proud to make it obvious, which is why he'd never acknowledged me before. This made me all the more determined to show him that I cared about him, to make it clear that I was there for him. The next night I had to stay late at work for stocktaking. I rushed home as quickly as I could and ran to the window, still clutching my bag and keys. His light wasn't on, he was usually in at that time. I took off my coat and sat in my red chair, which had long since been moved to the window. I sat there until four in the morning, but he didn't come. He must've been there earlier and was punishing me for not being there.

After that, I always refused to stay behind. I was in the middle of this story about my mother having lung cancer and I was about to say that I had to visit her every night, when I remembered I'd once told Monica that she lived in Morecombe, so I had to say that I had to phone her at six every night, and it became quite a feeble excuse. I should've just said that she'd moved.

'That's terrible,' consoled Monica. 'Especially when she doesn't even smoke.' I'd forgotten she'd met her once in the Cottage Café when she was up on a visit. Every day they would ask me how she was. I would spend my time trying to avoid people so that I didn't have to talk about it. I just didn't care, so long as I got to see him every night. I was determined to keep him interested, terrified that he might just get bored with me. I was constantly buying new clothes and make-up. I did facial exercises. I tried curling my hair, I tried straightening my hair. I bought a blonde wig. I stopped eating. But he was there less and less. I knew he wanted more.

I carefully applied some Hot Amour red lipstick, I don't usually wear anything other than dusky pink or the occasional plum, and covered my eyes with dark blue glittery eye-shadow together with some false eyelashes, that preferred to stick to my fingers rather than my eyelids, but eventually I managed to get them balanced precariously in roughly the right place. I was ready to dress. I put on some lacy black underwear that Donald had once given me for Christmas, with my red floppy kimono draped loosely over my shoulders. I then put on my wig and teased the blonde curls so that they fell around my face and added some diamante earrings to complete the look – and a red light-bulb. I then just had to wait. I sat in my chair and leant my cheek against the window, finding the coldness of the glass calming against my face. 'What are you doing?' I began to ask myself when his light came on across the way. It was ten to six, he was earlier than usual, he must've seen the red light. He appeared and stood against the window. I also stood and we looked at each other for just a moment. I then turned around so that I had my back to him and let my kimono fall to the floor as I had seen happen in many a film. I turned to face him in my skimpy underwear and I began to slip off the straps of my all-in-one. The cold was bringing out goose pimples along my arms. I let the material fall past my breasts. I glanced at my watch, he had been there for five minutes and ten seconds already. I pulled the underwear completely from my body and stood there naked and cold, not sure what to do next, as this was all I had planned. I closed my eyes and became aware of the Neighbours theme-tune drifting up from downstairs. I slowly slid my hand between my legs and began to rub myself gently. I let myself get carried further and further away until nothing but silence filled my head. I could feel myself getting hotter as I rubbed harder and faster, letting my body swell with pleasure. I started to groan out loud. I opened my eyes to share the moment with him and he had gone. I noticed the young boy across the way peering at me curiously from his bedroom window. I quickly pulled the curtains shut.

The next day at work Monica ran into the staff room and said that she had just taken a message that my mother had been rushed into hospital with suspected stomach cancer.

'I thought she was already in hospital,' she squawked.

'I must go to Morecombe,' I answered.

Ten minutes later a taxi arrived and I stumbled into the back in a half dream-like state, trying to take the news in.

'I just want to go to the station.' I started rummaging through my purse to check I had enough money for my train fare.

'Going anywhere nice?'

'Just to my mother's,' I replied, not looking up. 'She's sick.' I hoped he would leave it at this; it was obvious that I was upset.

'I hope it's nothing serious. My Auntie has just been in hospital with her bladder.' His voice was slow and flat and very irritating. His slowness seemed to grate with the panic that I felt inside. I had thirty-two pounds, that was plenty. I glanced up to see where we were, when I noticed the back of his neck. Something about it seemed familiar, so did the dark T-shirt and the greased hair.

'She had terrible trouble with it. What time's your train?' I couldn't quite catch my breath.

'Two,' I managed to squeak. It couldn't be, I thought. I suddenly felt very sick. I wanted to jump out but I needed to get to the station. I opened the window slightly and let the rain spit on my face. I'm being stupid, I thought, it can't be him. The lights were on red. We sat there in silence. I couldn't stop looking at the back of his neck. I wanted to scream. I prayed he wouldn't look round.

'It's been quiet today. I've been a taxi driver for seven years and I've never known it as quiet as it has been lately. People haven't got the money for taxis anymore. To tell you the truth I'm a bit sick of it now anyway, I wouldn't mind getting out of the game if I could.' I listened to his voice drone on and on. 'It's quite a good job really but I'm sick of sitting down. When I get home the last thing I want to do is sit down so I stand up. I watch TV standing, I read standing, I'll even eat my dinner standing up.' Another red light. 'It's the family joke that I eat standing up. We all go to my Mum's on Sunday for dinner and if I'm working in the afternoon I'll even stand to eat my Sunday dinner. I know a lot of other drivers feel like me about sitting down.' Luckily we had just turned into the station forecourt.

'How much do I owe you?' I asked quickly, as we drew to a halt.

'Let me see. That's two pounds and ten pence.' I threw him a fiver and threw myself from the taxi, catching my foot in the seat belt on the way. He ran round to help me as I lay sprawled on the pavement, wishing that I would just die there and then. He took my arm and pulled me to my feet, he looked right into my eyes but he didn't seem to recognise me. For the first time, I noticed he was wearing glasses.

'You forgot your change, love. You alright?' I nodded. 'Take it easy on your trip.' He laughed and ran round to the driver's side, climbed in and drove away.

Two days later I arrived home. Luckily it had only been an ulcer. I walked into my dark room and quickly pulled the curtains shut before I put the light on. The room seemed different somehow. I suddenly noticed my weeping fig was lying thrown across the carpet and, where my television had been, there was just an empty space. I stood there trying to take it in, not knowing what to do. It was so cold. I switched on the electric bars of the fire and dragged my chair in front of it where I sat huddled in my duffel coat.

Summer 1957 - Dream of the Desert

Valérie Olek

Titi was sitting on the mat, under the blue parasol. A warm wind from the desert was blowing sand on the beach and pushing waves back from the shore. Titi watched her cousins play on the rocks and fight for little crabs in the pools. They were about the same age, but Titi felt quite estranged with the two boys. She had been with them for one week and had not got used to their loud voices, their funny 'Pied-Noir' accent and their restlessness. She remembered with a shiver how on her first day they locked her in the toilets, a little wooden cabin near a large fig tree in the courtyard. Pushing against the door to prevent her from coming out, they started shouting that the big snake was going to come and eat her. Luckily her Auntie Palmyre arrived like a tornado and started hitting her sons with the silver ladle she always kept at hand. There was indeed a snake in the fig tree and sometimes it came into the toilets. Titi found many things strange in this country.

Her mother had sent her to Algiers for three months of summer holidays. She thought that Titi was pale and that the sun of Algeria and the air of the seaside would do her good after a dull Parisian spring. Palmyre was her mother's older sister. A very affectionate woman, she was always ready to press the children against her ample bosom. She was also quick to beat the children with her silver ladle. She had not had an easy life. Her husband had left her and their two sons years ago; she had to struggle to bring them up. She also had to raise her younger brother, Titi's uncle Roger. He was now twenty-five but he still lived at Palmyre's house in La Roberceau, a quiet suburb of Algiers. Titi was at once most impressed by her uncle. A very tall, dark man, he seemed to listen to the radio all day. He did no work; he was an experimenter... Auntie Palmyre explained that he had had a bad fall the previous year because of his attempt to fly. He had jumped from the balcony with an open umbrella. Luckily he had only broken his nose... and the umbrella. Uncle Roger also dressed up as Tarzan, to go fishing on the rocks at dawn. He fastened a grass skirt around his hips and took a long spear he had made. For Titi he was a kind of hero.

It became very warm on the beach and Titi decided to have a swim. The beach was empty. It was just after lunch and most people were at work or having a nap in the coolness of their houses. Auntie Palmyre gave oranges to Titi and the boys for lunch. She did not want them to have heavy stomachs when they were spending a day on the beach. To Titi these oranges were delicious compared to those of France, almost like a different fruit. She loved as well the strange seedy figs and pomegranates she had discovered here.

The sea was warm and clear. Titi walked on the multicoloured pebbles and had a swim. But she was cautious. This part of the coast was known for its strong undercurrents and, every year, some people from France drowned there, Auntie Palmyre had warned her.

As she returned to the parasol, her cousins left the rocks with two green plastic buckets.

'Come on Titi,' said Jacques, the older boy, putting on his sandals, 'we are going home'. They rolled the mats, closed the parasol and walked slowly on burning sand to the cliff path. The house was just on top. It had been built by Titi's great-grandfather, when he first arrived in Algiers from his village in Italy. It was a big white house with three floors. Auntie Palmyre and the boys were living on the ground floor while Uncle Roger stayed on the second. The third floor was rented to Mr and Mme Coulon, an elderly couple who argued continually. They often threw pans, plates and all sorts of things from the window and you had to be careful not to be stunned by a flying plant pot when sitting in the courtyard. However, Auntie Palmyre did not want them to go because they were never late paying the rent.

The boys had walked quickly to the house and Titi was the last to enter the courtyard. To her surprise, a girl was sitting on the floor podding green beans. She wore a purple dress and her curly black hair lay loose on her shoulders. She raised her head and the two girls looked at each other.

They were the same age. Titi dropped the mats on the floor.

'Hi,' she said. 'What are you doing?'

'I am helping my mama,' the other one replied. Titi understood that she was Fatma's daughter; Fatma was the house help of her Auntie. Three days a week she came to do housework for the family. She was a big woman, always wrapped in a white gown. Titi thought she was beautiful; little green tattoos on her forehead, the palms of her hands dyed orange. Auntie Palmyre always said that Fatma was lazy and often shouted at her. Even now, Titi could hear the loud voice of her Auntie in the kitchen.

'I can help you,' proposed Titi, sitting down beside the girl. She pulled the pan near her and grabbed a few beans. The other girl looked surprised but said nothing.

'By the way, I'm Titi, Jacques' and Paul's cousin. What's your name?'

'Salima,' the dark girl answered. Titi could see Salima was afraid of the shouting coming from the house. She kept turning her head towards the kitchen window.

'She is nice but she always shouts,' Titi said with a smile. 'Yesterday I thought she was going to kill Paul because he had taken her dear silver ladle to unblock the toilets!'

Salima laughed. As they finished the beans, Auntie Palmyre came out of the house with two large pieces of bread rubbed with olive oil and garlic for them. Fatma also came to put some newly washed clothes on the line. She called Salima sharply in Arabic and the girl stood up to help. She looked frail beside her imposing mother.

* * *

The noise of the cicadas was deafening in the night. The family had finished their evening meal. Uncle Roger was having a cup of coffee. Nobody talked, not even the boys. The news was bad. There had been several bomb attacks in town that day and Chez George, one of the most popular cafés on the main square, had been destroyed. There were many casualties. Auntie Palmyre cried after she heard the news from Mme Coulon. She still had red, puffy eyes and was sniffing.

'What are we going to do?' she asked finally, her voice

breaking. 'I am afraid to go to the shops or the cinema now. Anything can happen.' Nobody answered. She started again.

'You can't trust anyone anymore. Take Fatma, for example... Janie Coulon said her husband and son were Fellaghas!'

Titi and the boys shivered. They knew about the Fellaghas who put bombs in town and slaughtered people. Titi understood that they wanted French people to leave the country. It seemed unfair to the girl. Her family had built their own house here.

'Mme Coulon sees Fellaghas everywhere, 'Uncle Roger said with a smile. 'She thought that old Mohamed the ragman was one! He is bent like an old tree and can hardly push his wheel-barrow!'

'I like Mohamed!' Jacques screamed.

'Me too!' Paul shouted.

'Hush, children,' Auntie Palmyre whispered.'Don't get excited.' She stood up heavily and said to herself, 'I suppose we'll have to go to France.'

* * *

Titi woke up. She must have been sleeping under the parasol a long time, since the usual Saturday crowd had almost entirely left the beach. The wind was fresher and the light golden now. Auntie Palmyre sat in a low deckchair, reading a magazine. The ladle lay on the mat beside her, ready to be used if the boys were foolish. At present they seemed quiet, playing on the rocks.

'Are you alright, Titi?' she asked the girl. Titi nodded. She looked healthier after a few weeks. Her legs were brown and her hair was white as sand. She often thought it funny that Salima should be so pale. After all, she lived there all year long.

The two girls became friends. After their first meeting, Salima had returned with her mother. The two girls started helping her with the washing, or peeling fruit and vegetables. Titi was at once fascinated by Salima's family. She learnt that Salima's mother was called Ouria, not Fatma! Fatma was just a general name to call Arab women.

Salima had come to Algiers with her parents and brother from a village near the desert, while the rest of the family stayed. Salima said that they were not poor but that life was harder there.

Two weeks before, Salima had invited Titi home. Auntie Palmyre had been reluctant at first, but Titi was very convincing. Fatma and Salima came for Titi in the afternoon. They caught the bus to town, then walked to the high town, the white Casbah on the hill of Algiers. The walk was exhausting. The narrow streets were steep and crowded with children playing, men sitting on their heels in the doorways or standing in little groups. At last they arrived. Ouria entered an open door into a dark, fresh room. The girls sat on the carpet and ate honey, almond and orange flower cakes. Titi smelled in the room the same perfumes as in Ouria's and Salima's hair. Later, Salima's father came into the house, a tall man dressed in white with warm dark eyes. He did not talk much.

After that evening, Titi went back several times to her friend's home. She was shown how to roll the couscous semolina with the palms of her hands, or to knead the bread, or just to blow in the little flute of Salima's brother. Ahmed could play magic tunes on this flute, tunes that made his father bend his head and his mother cry. Ahmed worked as an apprentice in a jewellery workshop. At first he had completely ignored Titi but gradually he got used to seeing the blonde girl around.

Titi was now dreaming in front of the sea. She liked to be at Salima's house. It was so different from Auntie's, from everyone else she knew. She sometimes wanted to live with them. She and Salima had made plans. They could go for a while to the village of Salima's family. But how could she tell Auntie Palmyre? And Maman? How could she tell them she wanted to wear a coloured gown and live in the desert? That she wanted the same green tattoos as the Arab women?

Auntie Palmyre stood up and started packing. She called Jacques and Paul, who pretended not to hear. She called again with a louder voice and shook the silver ladle over her head with a menacing expression. This time the two boys made a move. Titi helped her Auntie roll the mats and the beach towels, and they walked home.

* * *

There were now bomb attacks almost every day, at the post office, in the cinemas or the cafés. The police launched round-ups in the Casbah. People were afraid, suspicious but, strangely, still wanted to live as before. They refused to see that it was just a question of time... Auntie Palmyre, pushed by Janie Coulon, was on the back of Fatma all the time. But she did not dare to shout at her any longer. There had been the terrible case of that maid slaughtering a family recently.

Then, one morning, Fatma came with Salima to say goodbye. They were going back to the village. Titi cried a lot. All her dreams of going to the desert were collapsing. Salima was sad too; she gave Titi a little pendant. It was the open hand of the Fatma, symbol of luck. Her brother Ahmed had made it in his workshop.

* * *

Auntie Palmyre took Titi to a large shop in town. Despite her fear of attacks she wanted to buy some presents for Titi to take home. As they wandered round, Titi's attention was attracted by a dark youth with a small bag on his shoulder. Coming nearer to him she realised it was Ahmed. He was looking at a display of scarves and had dropped the bag at his feet.

Suddenly the shop was full of screaming and shouting as several policemen came running through the alleys. Titi looked around. Ahmed had gone but his bag was still on the floor. She had just enough time to seize it before the shop was evacuated in a complete panic. People were pushing one another to get out. It was a bomb alert. Still holding the bag firmly against her, Titi came out of the shop. She had lost Auntie Palmyre. The policemen kept pushing people away and, just as Titi was reaching the opposite side of the road, a terrible explosion blew up the shop. Everybody dived on the pavement. After a few seconds of deadly silence, shouts, cries and screams started filling the street. People stood up, trying to find friends or relatives.

Several police vans arrived with howling sirens. Titi stood up too. She was shaking. She wanted to find her Auntie.

As she crossed the road she saw a crowd near a police van and she walked towards it. Two policemen were holding an Arab. He was badly beaten up. Titi recognized Ahmed. His headscarf was full of blood, his arm twisted behind his back by a policeman. She heard people say that he was the one who had put the bomb in the shop. He was seen with a bag by a shop assistant. Titi suddenly realised that she still had Ahmed's bag. She pushed her way through and grabbed the arm of a police officer, trying to explain. After a moment of confusion the man understood the girl. He seized the bag and opened it... It contained only the carving and jewellery tools of the young man. Ahmed had seen Titi but turned his head away. The policemen let go of him without a word, gave him his bag and pushed him. The crowd became silent as the staggering young man walked away. As he reached the end of the street, Ahmed turned back and waved timidly to Titi. The girl touched the Fatma's hand pendant and watched him disappear around the corner.

The crowd had dispersed by now. Titi saw Auntie Palmyre, sat in the middle of the street, crying, her head in her hands. She ran towards her.

Straight Grain

Julie Lerpiniere

Only when the final bruise had faded to a faint brown ring beneath her right eye did Laurel manage to find the courage to set foot outside the refuge alone. She was surprised to find it was already late summer. The trees which lined the avenue were beginning to turn, their foliage tinged with yellow ochre and sienna – here and there a leaf drifted down onto the grass verge – and their heavy trunks threw long thick shadows across the road, cast by a lowering sun.

The air was still, dense and warm and fragranced with the scents of privet, roses, hot tarmac and woodsmoke. It was the woodsmoke which told Laurel it was almost autumn, the aroma instantly transporting her back to her childhood and those bonfires of garden rubbish she and her mother would burn on chilly September evenings. She thought of the cheery carefree child she had been then and wondered again how she'd ever got herself into this mess, and how the hell she was ever going to get out of it.

Conscious that each step was taking her further from the security of the refuge, Laurel made her way slowly and deliberately up the avenue. She reached the main road and paused, leaning against a garden wall until the panic attack passed. Then, still trembling, but breathing more easily she turned left and headed for the shops.

It being Wednesday afternoon and therefore half-day closing, only the newsagents was open. Relieved at having been spared the agonies of a crowded butcher's, baker's and greengrocer's, Laurel went in and bought a pint of milk, a Walnut Whip and the local evening paper.

She ate the Walnut Whip in the nearby park. Perched at the very end of a low concrete bench, she tore off the wrapper with clumsy nervous fingers and crammed the confection quickly into her mouth, finishing it in three bites, barely tasting the chocolate or fondant filling, but licking her fingers afterwards anyway. Then she sat back and, closing her eyes, tried to account for the lost weeks between now and the last time she'd been out alone. That had been back in April – a raw night with a bitter wind blowing stinging rain into her face, numbing her hands and making her coat and headsquare flap wildly about her as she waited at the lonely bus stop, bleak and desolate.

Laurel remembered the bus stop. She didn't remember getting there, she didn't remember the journey to the hospital, or her wounds being tended. She remembered hot sweet tea, clean bandages, a smell of antiseptic and a firm gentle voice telling her that this was the last time such a thing would happen, because she was going away, a long way away, where he wouldn't be able to find her. And so she woke in a strange house in a strange city in the company of a group of strange women, with only the clothes she'd arrived in to call her own.

There followed weeks of interviews and meetings – social services, DHSS, solicitors – and here she was, the whole summer gone unnoticed; winter drawing near, with no home other than the refuge, no money other than her benefits, no clothes other than those pulled out of the 'charity bag', no job, no friends and no future.

'Well, that takes care of the story so far,' thought Laurel, 'now what next I wonder?' And in an effort to distract herself from the enormity of the task of gathering up the pieces and rebuilding her life once more, she opened the evening paper and began to flick through it.

Laurel returned to find the refuge unusually silent. She wiped the crumbs from the kitchen table, did a pile of washing up, made herself tea and toast and, perching on one of the uncomfortable plastic stools at the formica 'breakfast bar', opened the Evening News and once more pulled out the supplement entitled 'New Horizons - Community Education Classes for Adults'. Frowning, Laurel ran a buttery fingertip down the list of subjects, pausing at some, then moving on, disregarding others without so much as a second glance.

By the time she'd eaten her toast and drained her mug of tea, she'd made a decision. She took a pen and ringed the relevant information. Then she read it again. 'Dressmaking,' it said. 'Wednesday evenings 7p.m. - 9p.m.

Enrolment 10th Sept. 6p.m. - 8p.m. St. Hilda's Centre, Spring Bank.' Six till eight. Laurel checked her watch. Better get a move on or she'd be late and the class may be full. She washed her face, changed her blouse and was just leaving when the others returned.

Reaching the community centre was easier than Laurel had anticipated. She'd only had one panic attack on the corner of Park Avenue and Spring Bank, outside the Old Brass Bell. There had been no-one around to notice and she'd collected herself, wiped her sweaty palms with a freshener tissue and forced herself along the road, across the car park and into the centre.

Inside St Hilda's it was hot, airless and heaving with people. Laurel's courage almost failed her but she gritted her teeth, clenched her fists and made herself approach the reception desk. Her feet felt like concrete blocks, her legs like fraying rope. Each step seemed to take an age.

'Hello,' said the woman behind the desk pleasantly. 'How can I help you?'

'Dressmaking please.' Laurel's voice was little more than a whisper. The woman gave her a form.

'Fill this in,' she said, 'and take it down the corridor to the last room on the right.'

Laurel did as she was told. She was good at doing as she was told. Sometimes it had averted a beating. Only sometimes. Laurel shuddered, shut off the memory and concentrated on checking she had the right documents for enrolment. Then she joined the queue and hoped no-one had noticed how much her hands were shaking.

'Hi!' said a jolly voice behind her. 'This the queue for dressmaking?'

Laurel swung round, startled. Grinning cheerily at her was a smallish woman of average build with short hennaed hair and crow's feet at the corners of twinkling grey eyes. She wore jeans, pumps, a black T-shirt emblazoned with an abstract design in fluorescent colours, and huge vibrant dangling earrings. Laurel felt tall, gangling and drab next to her.

'Um yes,' she replied. 'Dressmaking. Yes. I think so.'
'You been before?'
'No. Have you?'

'No. I'm a complete novice. Glad I won't be the only one. I'm Alison, by the way.'

'Laurel.'

'Pleased to meet you.'

Alison chatted pleasantly to Laurel while they waited their turn, distracted her while she enrolled, and distracted everyone while she herself enrolled.

As she was so friendly Laurel felt obliged to wait for Alison, and so they left the building together. Alison offered Laurel a lift home but she declined, partly because she didn't want to reveal the address of the refuge, partly because she didn't want Alison to know she was living in a Women's Aid refuge, but mostly because she needed some time to assess the evening's events. Alison shrugged amiably.

'Suit yourself,' she said. 'Nice evening for a walk anyway. Right then. See you at class next week.'

'Bye,' said Laurel, and turned out of the gate and set off down the road, feeling the gentle warmth of the late summer sun on her face and arms and enjoying it for the first time in what seemed like forever.

When she got in, the other women were all in the lounge watching TV. Where had she been, they wanted to know. Laurel told them. Oh! they said. And why hadn't she mentioned it earlier, or invited any of them to come along? 'Because,' said Laurel bravely, 'I wanted to see if I could do it on my own. And I could.' One of the women got up and gave her a hug which made her cry, so someone else put the kettle on and made them a nice cup of tea.

A hobby is a luxury a woman can ill afford when struggling to survive on state benefits. Laurel's euphoria from signing up for her sewing class soon evaporated when she realised the price of patterns and fabric – prices far beyond the meagre sum she allowed herself for spends. She was seriously considering cancelling her enrolment when one of the support workers, Carol, came to the rescue.

'My sister was going to make this,' she explained, handing Laurel a Hammonds carrier bag, 'but she got pregnant so abandoned it in favour of maternity dresses. Don't know why she gave it to me, I can't tell one end of a needle from another. Can't bear waste, I suppose. Neither can I. So if it's any good have it.' Laurel opened the carrier bag and her eyes grew wide with surprise and delight. Inside was a generous length of charcoal grey wool suiting, matching taffeta lining and a brand new pattern for a neat straight skirt with a kick pleat at the back, and a short boxy double breasted jacket.

'You'll have to buy a zip and some buttons,' said Carol apologetically. Laurel shook her head dismissively. She was too busy marvelling over the fabric to worry about details like haberdashery. The wool felt soft and light in her fingers. She pulled it out of the bag and draped it over her shoulder. It fell gracefully to her ankles, hanging in elegant even folds.

'It's beautiful!' she said.

'The colour suits you,' said Carol, smiling. Laurels's pale cheeks flushed and her blue eyes sparkled. Even her mousy hair seemed to take on a new coppery lustre. She squeezed Carol's hand.

'Thanks,' she said, 'you don't know how much this means to me.' And folding the fabric carefully, she slid it back into the carrier and took it up to her room, where she placed it carefully on top of the chipboard and teak veneer wardrobe.

'Hello there!' called out Alison as Laurel stepped hesitantly into the community centre's craft workshop. Alison was at the far end of a large light airy room with tall windows down one side through which poured bright September evening sunshine. Beneath the windows was a long bench on which stood a number of electric sewing machines and a couple of strange looking gadgets Laurel was later to learn were overlockers. In the centre of the room were two large tables around which Alison and a group of other women were busily unpacking bags and sewing boxes. Opposite the windows was a row of built-in cupboards at the end of which was a full length mirror and a screen for fitting. Alison patted the chair next to hers.

'Come and sit here,' she said. 'Plenty of room. What are you making?' Laurel stared at the array of patterns and materials the women were heaping onto the table in silent amazement, fighting the desire to pick up and finger each piece of cloth, see how it felt, how it fell, how it swung, how it hung, and to take and examine each pattern closely and imagine it made up in her size. Because she could imagine them all made up in her size, and knew immediately which would suit her tall gaunt frame and which wouldn't. This revelation so surprised her that she had a panic attack and had to sit down, clutching her carrier bag with white knuckled fingers until it passed. Alison fetched her a cold drink from the vending machine in the corridor and patted her shoulder reassuringly.

'I used to have them,' she said briefly, 'but they passed. What's in your bag?' So Laurel showed her and she raised her eyebrows and gave a low whistle of admiration.

'Classy stuff,' she said. 'I'm impressed.' And she showed Laurel the Supa-simple pattern for Bermuda shorts and the cheap loud multicoloured cotton she had brought along. And they both laughed.

By the time the suit was finished Laurel had managed to scrape together enough money to buy some fabric for a blouse. So she arranged with Alison to spend a day at the market in the nearby town, where Alison knew of a stall selling cheap material.

It was a damp drizzly Saturday morning in November, a typical grey Northern morning, reflected Laurel as she trudged up the avenue, avoiding puddles and squelching over clumps of dead leaves, now trodden into a dirty brown mull that gave off an aroma of defeat and decay.

Alison was early. She drew up at the kerb-side just as Laurel reached the main road. Alison drove a sage green Morris Traveller with original wood panelling and no safety belts. Laurel climbed into the passenger side, sat down and immediately sank so far into the seat that her knees were level with her chin and her chin level with the dashboard. She also discovered that there was no handle inside the door with which to close it. Unperturbed, Alison got out, ran round, shut her in, ran back and jumped gaily behind the wheel. The windscreen wipers whirled busily and the engine chugged in a brisk, businesslike way, patiently awaiting instructions. Alison slipped the car into gear and they set off, trundling steadily up the road, Alison chatting happily all the way.

Much to Laurel's surprise (and relief) they reached the market and parked without incident. Alison took her for a coffee and then led her to Sophies, the material stall known to all dressmakers in the region as a source of cheap good quality fabrics. Laurel hadn't really had a clear idea of what to expect, but was totally unprepared for what she saw. The stall consisted of four trestle tables arranged in a hollow square in the middle of which stood Sophie, wrinkled and gnarled and stooping, measuring, cutting, taking money and talking constantly. On the tables, heaped as high as Sophie's rounded shoulders were fent upon fent of fabric in a bewildering array of colour, texture and pattern, which the surrounding crowd of women were pulling, tugging, feeling, examining, throwing back and haggling over. Alison grabbed Laurel's trembling hand and dragged her forward.

'Come on,' she said, 'let's get in on this free-for-all!'

At length Laurel settled on a burgundy grey and navy paisley in fine viyella for chilly days and a bright red polka dot print in light cotton viscose for summer. Two for the price of one. Laurel smiled with satisfaction.

They went back to Alison's for tea. Alison lived alone in a tiny attic flat at the top of a three-storey terraced house, a few streets away from the refuge. Laurel drifted from room to room while Alison organised some food. There was a bedroom, living room/kitchen and toilet.

'Where's the bathroom?' asked Laurel.

'Here,' said Alison and pulled aside a plastic curtain in the kitchen to reveal a short but deep bathtub.

'Well I never!' exclaimed Laurel and they both laughed.

Alison had furnished the flat with bits and pieces she'd picked up from flea markets and jumble sales. Nothing matched, from the oak wardrobe and pine dressing-table in the bedroom to the lumpy settee and huge overstuffed armchair in the living room, over which she'd thrown old dyed bedspreads and lengths of bright fabric. Rag rugs lay across the bare boards and everywhere were china and glass jugs and plates and vases. Postcards in clip frames hung in clusters on all the walls, and plants were everywhere, hanging from the ceiling, perched on shelves and window sills, sitting with smug satisfaction on the floor by the lavatory and the side of the single gas fire in the living room. Laurel looked out of the window, set deep into the slanting slate roof. It overlooked the park and in the gathering dusk she could just make out bare trees and muddied grass. A street lamp came on, its halo of light made hazy by the persistent drizzle. It looked bleak and forlorn. But inside Alison's flat it was different. It was warm and snug and welcoming. Alison came through with a glass of wine. In her wake drifted the aroma of hot garlic bread, wholemeal pasta and pesto sauce. Laurel accepted the wine and decided Alison was the most marvellous woman she'd ever met, which made her wonder why she should choose her as a friend. She thought about asking but was too afraid to, so instead she followed Alison into the kitchen and offered to set the table.

The following morning, at the refuge, Laurel waited until everyone had finished breakfast. Then she cleared the table and washed up. Next she painstakingly ironed the paisley viyella, spread it across the table-top and pinned the blouse pattern to it, taking care to keep them on the straight grain of the fabric. Whilst making the suit Laurel had learned about straight grain. She'd also learned about interfacing, lining, button-holing and overlocking. And she'd learned fast. So fast in fact that her tutor had suggested she think about taking the City and Guilds certificate in dressmaking. Laurel thought about it as she slowly and precisely cut into her material. She thought she might give it a try.

Around the middle of April, winter grudgingly gave way to spring. Nights became lighter, the air milder, the breeze warmer, the rain softer. Birds returned from southerly climes and began to nest in the trees in the park, which now sported brave tight buds. Crocuses thrust white and purple heads and stubby green leaves up towards a pale sun, and daffodils swayed and nodded in a yellow waxy chorus-line along the sides of footpaths. Laurel was offered a flat by the local housing association and so postponed her plans for shorts and summer frocks while she made cushion covers and bedding.

Alison helped her move in. There wasn't much to move; a bed, wardrobe, chest of drawers, cooker, fridge and table bought with a single payment from the DHSS, a few bits and pieces she'd acquired from charity shops and, in pride of place, the old treadle sewing machine she'd picked up for a fiver at a flea market the previous month. The wooden case was stained, scratched and chipped and the wrought-iron frame a little rusted, but the machine itself was in full working order. Laurel loved it and had taken to sewing on it in the early hours of the morning when recurrent nightmares denied her sleep, finding the rocking motion of the treadle soothing and comforting.

The following week Sophie offered Laurel a part-time job serving on her stall on Wednesdays and Fridays, cash in hand, no questions asked, and with her first wages she bought a battered old two-seater sofa, which she covered in navy blue cotton drill, catterin chintzy and floral cushions in blues, greens and sunshine yellow across the back, adding a crisp white linen and lace antimaccassar – also from a flea market – to complete the effect. With her next wages she bought two sturdy dining chairs, two wine glasses and another plate, and invited Alison for tea.

Alison arrived early in the pouring rain. Laurel answered the door to find her grinning and dripping water from her earrings, her cagoule and her hennaed hair, which clung to her cheeks and neck in fine copper strands.

'Hope you don't mind me coming early,' she said in a muffled voice, as Laurel vigorously towelled her hair dry, 'but I've got this pattern and material for a fitted top and it's all a bit tricky so I thought you might cut it out for me and help me decipher the instructions.'

'Of course I will,' said Laurel, flattered at being asked. 'It'd be a pleasure.'

Alison gratefully handed the carrier bag full of sewing to her and went to put the kettle on. Laurel opened the bag, gasped and followed her into the kitchen.

'Alison, this is silk,' she said wonderingly, lovingly running the smooth oyster fabric through her fingers. 'Are you sure you want to trust me with it?'

'Course I do,' replied Alison without hesitation. 'You're my best friend. If I can't trust you, who can I trust?'

Moved, Laurel bit her lip to stop herself from crying, then turned briskly and spread the silk on the table and began to arrange the pattern pieces onto it.

'Alison,' she said, without looking up, 'I've been wanting to tell you. Where I lived before was a Women's Aid refuge. I'm a battered wife.'

'Was,' said Alison smiling, 'not any more.' She poured the tea.

'You're not shocked?'

'No. I knew anyway. I could tell.'

'How?'

'Because I was a battered wife too until a couple of years ago.'

'You!' cried Laurel in astonishment, 'but you're wonderful! How did you...?'

'You never forget,' interrupted Alison gently, 'but you do get beyond it. And eventually, you learn to pick up the pieces and rebuild your life. And you make sure that this time it's one worth having.'

A life worth having. Laurel glanced out of the open window. It had stopped raining and the sun was breaking through. The breeze carried in a sharp scent of wet leaves and moist earth. It smelled rich and vibrant and hopeful. Laurel placed the final pattern piece on the straight grain of the oyster silk, pinned it and began to cut.

Mascara

Paul Morris

Rain streaks across the windows of the train and I pass the time placing bets on the racing drops. The hills unfold behind the drizzle like someone shaking out a khaki blanket. London's elastic tide of flotsam and pollution ebbed from around the train hours ago and my mind feels empty as a virgin beach. As the hills approach I can make out the intimate rusted twists of the mine scaffold below them. Corrugated iron sheets seem to hang from the structures like slipped trapeze artists, forced to contemplate the ground before their grip finally fails.

I used to live here, but left a little after we found the foreman's cat. It was strung up from the lamp-post outside his house. A noose of electrical cable choked it as it fought to escape, yanked harshly back to this life in occasional spasms. Finally it died with a reflexive ripple of its tail. I slumped in the gutter gagging, but my elder brother William watched in fascination as the cat turned lazily in the cold air with one leg pointing stiffly out like a compass-needle.

That afternoon William and me sat on the slag heap above the mine. We tossed black shale over the cliff edge into the quarry below. It made a satisfying 'gloop' sound and the opaque green water rippled outward like creases in silk. The clatter and intermittent bangs of the mine were like a thin grey wash over the hills but somehow the racket was more peaceful than the deathly hush when the winding gear stopped.

The men burst from the lift shaft into the open air. Two punched each other playfully but their laughter was uneasy. When they came off the shift their faces were like a mask, greasy black from the coal dust smeared into their pores. Only their eyelids were blinked white. We skidded down the slag and stood outside the shower blocks, glancing furtively about for the foreman. William picked a fag-end off the ground and lit it with Mum's lighter, cupping his hand to cover the flame in the gathering dark. Inside, the men's voices echoed above the hiss of the water and we copied their obscenities.

'You're a fookin' bender, Bill, and so's your fookin' girlfriend.'

'I 'aven't even got one, ya shittin' scab.'

William grinned at me in expectancy. I rolled my eyes and bent down resignedly for him to put his foot in my interlocked hands. With a grunt I hoisted him up to the narrow windows of the block. I watched him in the fluorescent light, noticing how the fluff on his lip was becoming darker. His face was strangely cold.

Suddenly he hissed and dropped to the ground. We leaned against the wall, smoking nonchalantly. When the men emerged, their faces were scrubbed a stinging pink. But the coal dust still circled their eyelids in thin, ingrained rings, impossible to remove day after day.

'It's the showers what inverts 'em,' William muttered with a smirk. I shook my head slowly in confusion.

'You're a weird one, Bill Wakeley.'

When our Dad came out we ran alongside him and the others. I told him about the cat. The others suddenly fell quiet and looked at my Dad. He coughed and stared at the ground as he walked.

'Brimble's been job-timing us,' he said finally. 'For management. Could mean jobs'll go.'

The other men went into the pub but my Dad took us home silently.

The train clatters away leaving the valley silent. As I walk from the station the terraces seem to stare at their feet in the gutters. The sky is a blank grey and smoke-free now by law. In the town centre there is nothing much for the wind to whisper about. Few smells to carry except the grease of the doggedly persistent chip-shop on the corner and the heavy scents that curl about the doorway of Iqbal's grocers. As I walk by, their odours seem to slip suspiciously away. Last time I was here they mingled in the acrid smoke of coal fires.

A few lads lean outside the pub drinking and smoking. They watch me from across the street and I gaze back. One of them recognises me and the tension in his face melts into a curt nod. I shrug in my overcoat and turn into our street.

'How's work, son?'
'Much the same, Dad, y'know.'
He nods resignedly. The TV reflects electric blue light in his eyes. Mum potters about in the kitchen preparing my welcome-home roast. We sit in silence for a while in adjacent threadbare armchairs, both pretending to watch the news. Mum shouts from the kitchen over the tinny sliding of the joint into the oven's hissing inferno.
'Put your suit out if you want it ironing before tomorrow, son.'
My Dad shifts uneasily in his chair. I look at him for a moment then, with a sigh, push myself up from the armchair to go see if my Mum needs any help in the kitchen. She is standing motionless over the cooker staring at potatoes boiling in a pan. She seems to have shrunk and her face is thinner than I remember. Her hair is grey at the roots and darkens at the ends to tangled chestnut where she used to dye it. I go and put an arm around her shoulders and she weeps quietly for a while.
'It's okay, Mum,' I whisper. 'You're allowed to cry once a year.'

Soon after the cat, the strike came. William and me helped my Mum to take sandwiches to the pickets, wheeling them in an old shopping-trolley. The men whistled and cheered as we pushed the trolley up the hill, then made space around the brazier for us. They cracked jokes and put their arms around her to warm up and she smiled coquettishly. Like a glamorous French model, they said, and I noticed that for the first time in her life she was wearing no make-up.
As we trundled the trolley back down the hill to the baker's, William seemed quiet and distant. While we waited for Mum outside the shop, he grinned mischievously.
'He only gives us the bread 'cos she used to give 'im one when Dad were on nights,' he said, and stared at me. I glared at him and pointed to a sign on the door. It said 'Coal not

dole' in biro.

'Take that back now, Bill, 'cos *that's* why. He's one of us.'

William snorted and lit up a fag-end. I felt like smashing his face in, but Mum came out of the shop with the trolley stuffed full of loafs.

That night I woke to hear my Dad and William shouting at each other. The front door slammed and I looked out the window to see William walk into the night with his clothes stuffed in a carrier bag. I went to sleep listening to my Mum sobbing in the bedroom. Next morning he wasn't there for the sandwich run.

My Dad said nothing about the argument, and the way he stabbed his bacon with his fork stopped me from asking. My Mum's eyes were covered in make-up when we left the house but they still looked puffy and red. In a whisper she told me that William was living in a flat with a bloke called Ivor from the Council. They met on a solidarity demonstration in town. But I wasn't to let on to my Dad I knew.

We saw them later, William sharing fags with the pickets and Ivor standing quietly behind him, huddled up in a stolen NCB donkey jacket. William punched me on the shoulder and said, 'aw-right, our kid?' and Ivor smiled at me softly. My Mum sniffed as she hugged William and crumpled a five pound note into his hand, then turned quickly to push the trolley clattering down the hill. I trailed after her, glancing over my shoulder. William stood watching us with the money still clasped in his frozen fingers, until we went around a corner.

'William and Ivor must be good mates,' I said.

'That's right,' Mum said stiffly, 'and that's about all we've got left now.'

That was the last time I saw William. After they'd marched back for the last few yards of coal, the air heavy with declining profitability, my Dad started the drinking and the fighting. But there was a lot of that about, then.

Sticky tables and ash-speckled floor shudder to the throb of the music. Fluorescent lights, blue red green spin over a dance floor packed with naked entwined couples. There's this girl opposite me, legs twisted about mine. I can't remember where I've seen her before but she's laughing loud at everything I say. I strain to hear my own voice above the music. I'm reciting the tube stations on the Northern Line to work. Why does she find Finchley so funny? I lean forward to kiss her long neck but pull back in horror when I see she has a muffler made from a dead cat. It's twitching now and then.

William! He crosses the dance floor, pushing through the couples. William, no! But he can't hear me. He turns his head slowly and smiles. All black hair and blue eyes. He reaches out his hand to playfully tweak the bouncer's arse.

The girl pulls me by my hand, outside into the alley. Her muffler runs screeching into the night to reveal her naked body. I turn to see the bouncer leering as he cradles William's face in his big tattooed hands. I cannot move because my legs are made from a million tonnes of coal.

'Only a puff drinks lager,' the bouncer croaks as he licks his lips.

With the fist tattooed LOVE he punches William in the crotch. With the one marked MORE LOVE he throws him into the dirt. William waves to me as he falls and the bouncer kicks him over and over.

I wake to a sickly morning, clammy with sweat. I glance at my Buck Rogers radio-alarm and light a cigarette with shaking hands. It starts to rain softly outside and rivulets cascade down the slate roofs opposite, joining to form torrential rivers which will sweep me down through the streets and the hills back to London where I can drown in anonymous amnesia.

My Dad is gone by the time I go downstairs. My Mum smiles thinly as she puts out my breakfast, then hands me my suit on a hanger.

We walk arm in arm through the town under my Mum's umbrella. It is Sunday morning. We pick our way through last night's detritus, feet crunching on broken glass by the pub. Mum pauses under the little wooden arch of the church gate, listening to the people inside singing. The gravestones are blemished by the rain, odours of sodden soil and young grass loitering in the air, pungent as a narcotic. Greyish angels clamber over each other in ambiguous exaltation, raindrops clinging like lovers to withered petals. I feel sure that William would have liked it here, although he never was religious. Said we had enough denial imposed on us without volunteering for it as well.

While my Mum tends the flowers on William's grave I watch the people file out of the church. The priest looks like a great purple silk bat as he thanks them with a handshake and a practised smile. His smile slowly fades as he watches the last old couple shamble out through the gate, then makes his way slowly across the grass towards us.

My Mum shakes his hand weakly, her mascara blending with the make-up on her cheeks.

'Another year, is it?' he asks as he turns to me. 'Still, time means little to memory.' I gaze at his face, deliberately long and still. His hawkish good looks have slipped down to his jowls. His eyes flit away over the town.

'There must be a few changes since you were last here?' he asks. I nod and shrug.

'A few. Things have changed all over.'

'And not for the better.' He hisses through his teeth and points to a tomb with a headless angel. 'See that?' He shakes his head slowly. 'Must have been last night. Too many fishes in this little pond trying to make their mark. There's no heart in the place these days.'

He folds his hands behind his back and looks solemnly down at William's grave for a moment.

'You know, Jean, God's house can provide welcome shelter when a home provides little.'

My Mum draws herself upright and looks at him straight.

'It's not God my husband needs, Father, and neither does this town.'

We leave him with his decaying tombs.

We stop by at the pub on the way home. My Mum says she needs a drink but I know she is looking for my Dad. Inside, the barman washes up last night's empties and a few pasty-faced lads watch a burbling TV in the corner. I place her Cinzano on the table and slide onto the bench beside her. She sits and looks around her for a while. The wallpaper is nicotine yellow and peeling, the woodwork covered in thick crimson paint. There is a slight smell of disinfectant in the air.

'A miner himself, once, that bouncer,' she mutters and shakes her head.

I take a sip of my pint and try to summon up the bitterness I always feel after my recurring dream.

'Twenty-five years isn't long enough by half,' I spit.

She looks at me with a puzzled frown, then waves the cigarette she is about to light.

'Don't forget the violence was done to this place, son.' She draws on the cigarette heavily and her face is set so that the lines disappear and she could be young again. 'And when you can't fight back it's your own that sometimes end up getting hurt.'

In the corner the lads start laughing and singing along to *Songs of Praise* in mock piety.

As she unlocks the front door we hear the TV in the lounge. The door is ajar and I can see my Dad's body slumped across the sofa. She pushes the lounge door open.

The curtains are drawn. In the gloom my Dad is asleep with his mouth open and a bottle of Scotch on the floor next to his hand. Scattered next to the bottle are a mirror and one of my Mum's mascara brushes. I look at his face. Around his eyelids in thick, smudged black are two rings like coal dust.

My Mum shakes her head and stifles a giggle with a hand.

'You stupid old fool,' she murmurs, 'you stupid old fool. It's too late for that now!'

He is still asleep when I kiss my Mum goodbye at the front door.

The train is not due for hours so I walk down to the mine. I have to climb though a hole in the barbed-wire fence but everyone knows the guard-dog signs are a fake. I struggle up the waste heap, covered now with downy pubescent grass. My shoes slide into the shale and my legs begin to ache. A little further up a shadow straightens to watch me in the cold sun. It has a stuffed carrier bag in one hand. Then it bends again to pick for scraps of coal.

From the top I can see the winding gear and the green pool. I wonder why nobody has thought to knock it all down and smooth over the land with excavators, but what would replace it? It stands, slowly falling down, waiting for a change that never happened. Decaying, like my Dad, who could not change enough.

I find a big lump of coal in the new grass. I heave it up slowly into the cold blue sky and down it crashes into the green pool. The ripples spread outward steadily over all the surface and push softly at the edges.

The Visit

Fokkina McDonnel

The soldiers at the gate are joking and smoking. Some talk to a young woman. She smiles back uncertainly. Earlier today I joined a party of merchants and tradesmen. I keep in step with them. One walks on ahead and gives papers and passes, and perhaps bribes, to the armed men. Others hold up their bags and boxes to show the soldiers who wave them through. I follow closely. I keep my head down, averting my eyes. My hands rub my chin. In the shadows cast by the tower, dirt smeared on my face may pass for stubble. A small group of farmers returning from market makes its way in the opposite direction. I smell the afternoon heat, animals, fear. My sandalled feet want to rush on; I have to slow myself down deliberately.

I know every house, every alleyway, each signpost and doorway along the Via Rosa. I was born in this small city and lived here for nearly twenty years. Later, when I was homesick for it, I could turn to my dreams and see clearly the faces of my parents, my brothers, peeling plaster in the classroom, our goat, the cat. I would hear the small dogs and chatter of the women at the well, the echo of children's voices among trees. In these dreams I could even smell the leather, tobacco, spices of the shop next door and know that I belonged. Today, in the late afternoon, there are few inhabitants around. Are the others asleep or hiding? I hear no dogs, no children now. An old man appears from an alleyway. Is it Mr Adorno, our old neighbour? He briefly looks at me, then turns round. I want to go after him and ask him about my brothers. Where are they? Are they in the army? Are they still alive? Instead I touch the brick walls of our old home and feel no comfort. I mistimed my entry. I am trespassing.

Turning the corner at the Via Nova I see a small convoy of soldiers walking towards me. They are leading a group of young men blindfolded, stumbling. Folding my sleeve I slow down even further and affect a slight limp. Yes, I am safe – too old for prey. Many shops are already closed, or perhaps never opened today: fewer customers, searches several times a day. Soldiers sometimes take out their frustration on the old vendors, overthrow their market stall, set fire to the rugs painstakingly woven by mothers, aunts.

In the centre there are more people around. Here some banks and larger shops still do business. Men walk along the pavement. Well-dressed women with sunglasses talk about their purchases. On the main square the familiar plane trees catch the sun and whisper among themselves. This is where they string up traitors. Hold executions. For five minutes or so I make steady progress. Then the sound of guns shatters the stillness. Men and women around me startle, start to run, slip into doorways. My breath burns; I want to run with them to safety, but it might betray my disguise. I hobble on with my limp, shoulders tensing. There, at last, the doors of St. Maria Plena. For a few minutes I sit and pray. Light a candle. For him, for us. Specks of dust chase each other in the coloured light cast by stained-glass windows. In the yard a cat wakes up and blinks at me with green eyes, stretches and settles back to sleep. I pick up a broom and dreamily move dust, small stones from left to right, right to left, back and forwards. More gunshots are heard, further away. Like thunder, I count and feel safe from lightning. As the church bells call for Vespers, I move back into the street outside. Deserted now, except for some old women going to the service.

The rest of my journey passes without incident. As I enter the small shop my hand touches my hip. Feigning a limp is not easy and my bones ache. The owner, curled moustache, curled shoes, beckons me to the chair furthest away from him. Suddenly I understand; from underneath the white towels stick out two khaki legs, brown boots. Oh, my barber, drown the head now immersed in the washing bowl, slice the hairy neck, scalpel, splash blood like a sacrificial lamb to purify this small shop, turn it into an eternal sanctuary and refuge.

The barber rolls his large brown eyes and quickly, quietly I slip through a curtain into the alleyway. Out through the back into the yard. My body aches – with pain and longing. These journeys are becoming more dangerous each time.

Soon they may catch me and kill me. Torture me. I scratch on the door like a hungry mouse and tap on the window three times. My head rests against the rough and warm wood. Then the door opens and in the dark room, unmistakably, the odour of Atala, my lover and my husband. Holed up like a rabbit, he runs his troops from behind enemy lines. These army generals, majors, lieutenants visiting the best barber in town – if only they knew that the object of their desire sleeps and schemes, rests and plots a breath away.

An embrace, kisses, safety and adventure. Old terrain, new knowledge. I take out the parcels from underneath my robes. Vital information from our leaders and money, enough to support Atala until my next visit. We sing our song, return to the warmth of then, into and out past pain and pleasure. His stubble brushes my skin. Now his hands hold my hips. I, his queen, a woman turned an old wizened farmer. We whisper. Eat some bread, cheese and fruit. Talk of his needs, agree a date for my next visit. In my mind's eye I see myself wandering along the Via Rosa; a nun, a farmer again? Would carrying an animal be too risky? A travelling salesman? Then night comes and holds us safely.

From Suceava, you can hear the Wolves

Sylvia Christie

It was a long time ago; I was young and inexperienced. That was why they sent Dieter with me – he wasn't just an interpreter, he was a sort of minder. Poor Dieter – it wasn't his fault, what happened. I suppose it was mine. Mine and Jenna's.

Bucharest was cold and raw in the autumn of nineteen sixty-three. The cobbles were wet and the trees were bare, as bare as the trolley bus lines that traced the main streets. There wasn't much comfort there, between the monumental civic buildings and the great echoing churches – just a whistling wind, the clanking of the trolleys and a promise of snow from the north.

Dieter and I checked in at the hotel. It was as vast and impersonal as a town hall, but it had been a palace once. Royalty and the current jeunesse dorée had sipped cocktails and listened to the band where we slouched, weary from the flight, sipping *tsuica* with incredulity.

'By God, that's strong stuff,' I said. Dieter nodded. A man of few words. You'd never know he was fluent in seven languages. Including Rumanian, of course. That's why he was there. Only, he wasn't supposed to let anyone know he could understand the language. Industrial spying seems far too strong a term for it, but the philosophy was, play dumb, listen, and see what you can find out. Then, later, he could tell me what they'd been saying to each other, about our offers, about our deals.

Dieter wasn't much fun. He was older than I was, of course, and a settled family man.   He'd had enough excitement in his life during the war. I wasn't settled, I had an appetite for new things, new sights, new feelings. I'd left Gwen at home with the baby and the feeling I'd had, seeing her waving goodbye, was a mixture of guilt and relief. When that wore off, I knew I was ready for adventures.

In Bucharest, there didn't seem to be many adventures, with Dieter falling asleep over his dinner. I left him nodding and went down the broad, threadbare staircase, through the echoing foyer, past the reception desk where an elderly woman sat behind the oldest typewriter I had ever seen, and out into the street. There weren't many people about. I walked — rather quickly, to keep warm — down to the corner of the block. Two men in long black leather coats eyed me. I walked even faster back again.

There was a little kiosk opposite and I called in to buy cigarettes and matches. That was where I met Jenna.

She came in as I struggled to make myself understood. I caught her eye on me, as the man offered me pipe tobacco in a flimsy paper packet. When I refused an evil black cigar, and he threw up his hands in despair, she stepped in.

'You want cigarettes?' she asked me.

'Yes!' I was overwhelmed with pleasure. 'Can you help me? Are you English?'

'No, but I speak English a little,' she said. Her dark eyes suddenly beamed at me under an absurd red beret. 'I teach English at the Lycée.'

'That's wonderful,' I said. 'Can you ask him to sell me some cigarettes and a box of matches, please?'

A rattle of unknown words passed to and fro, and she turned back to me.

'Show me your money,' she said. I held out a handful of notes and she picked out one or two.

I offered her a cigarette, which she accepted.

'You are English?' she asked. 'You are tourist?' I shook my head.

'Business,' I said. 'I have business here — with your industrialists.' I was conscious of sounding important.

'Oh,' she said. 'That is interesting.' She wasn't impressed and I changed the subject. What she seemed to want was to practise her English and what I wanted, what I wanted more and more as I tried to talk to her, was to make her laugh, to make her pretty mouth curve upwards, to lose the frown that looked worried, though it might just have been puzzled. In the end, I invited her back to the hotel for a drink and she, politely but very firmly, refused.

'But perhaps we meet again,' she said. 'You travel soon?'

'Tomorrow,' I said. 'Tomorrow we go to Suceava, to one of the factories there.'

She shivered a little, in her heavy dark clothes. 'Suceava,' she said. 'I was born in Suceava. It is far in the hills.' She pointed to the north. 'From Suceava, you can hear the wolves.' The frown was back and the lips drooped.

'Didn't you like Suceava?' I asked.

Her face became blank.

'Is better here,' she said. It was time to change the subject again.

'We'll be back at the end of the week,' I said. 'Will you come to the hotel and have dinner with me then?'

'Dinner,' she said. Her eyes sparkled. I noticed how thin she was — not just slim, but thin. 'Thank you very much,' she said, stiltedly. 'I should be happy to accept.'

'Good,' I said. 'Friday at half-past seven, then.'

She smiled.

Our visit to Suceava was less than successful. Dieter and I made our way through fresh snow from the station; taxis were non-existent, but Dieter said the mill was within half a mile. I have never felt so cold in my life. I told Dieter about the wolves, but he simply grunted; then, after a few more frozen yards, he spoke.

'I wouldn't take much notice of the girl, if I were you,' he said. 'Out for what they can get, these women.' I was surprised at his surliness.

'She isn't a hooker, if that's what you mean,' I said. He only shook his head and we trudged on. I looked at the streets we passed — blocks of dingy flats, geometrically arranged, pierced by wide, empty, white roadways with a few ruts where sledges had been pulled. In the distance, there were hills, steep and wild, with dark pine forests on their slopes. The wind funnelled down through the flats from the north. I shivered. Jenna was right — it was better in Bucharest, comfortless though that might be. At least there was some evidence of past prosperity there — the monumental stone buildings and the ornate churches — and some sign of life in the clanging trolleys and snarling buses. Here, we might have been in a huge, abandoned penal colony, built for nothing but utility, fit for nothing human.

The factory was better. The warm familiarity of the smell of papermaking, the steamy vats of pulp — these were comforting, and the coffee in the manager's office was good.

Dieter took no part in the business. In theory, he was my assistant. They had provided their own interpreter, at my request, and Dieter merely sat in on the deal. We'd arranged that he'd rub his chin if he gathered from the conversation that something was being put over on me. By lunchtime, his chin was taking a fair bit of punishment, so I backed out as gracefully and ambiguously as I could.

'What was all that about?' I asked him. He shot a quick look round to see we were out of earshot.

'Not sure,' he said. 'I think – mind you, I only think – they were going to be selling the stuff on. Probably to the Russians.'

'I thought they didn't like the Russians?'

He shrugged. 'Not much choice,' he said.

'So, technically, we'd be selling to a middleman for the Russians?'

'Exactly.'

We were both silent. This was a no-go situation. However much the Company wanted eastern business – and heaven knew they wanted it badly – we couldn't allow this to happen. If it became public knowledge – if international affairs worsened – if – if – I sighed.

'Bit of a problem, then, Dieter? Good job you were there.'

He smiled, briefly.

'That's why they sent me.'

We got back to Bucharest next day, having politely broken off our negotiations with many promises of seeking information from Headquarters on both sides. We all smiled like the lying connivers we were. Nothing was said, but we knew, and they knew, that our state-of-the-art technology wouldn't be coming their way.

The hotel was almost like home, now. Dieter insisted on contacting the airline to try to get an earlier flight, but they had nothing till our booking on Monday. We had the weekend in Bucharest before us.

I wondered if Jenna would turn up on Friday night. She'd seemed to like the idea, but maybe she'd only been polite. She didn't really know me, any more than I knew her. I knew I wanted to know her better... At seven, I was in the foyer, sitting on worn red plush, watching the revolving doors.

She was still wearing her red beret on the shining black hair. Her feet were elegant in black patent, her thin body wrapped in thick dark wool. She smiled when she saw me.

I don't remember what we talked about. I remember her eyes, over a glass of wine; I remember her pleasure with a dish of pasta, her laughter at my attempts at a word or two in her complicated language, not quite French, not quite Italian. And afterwards, I remember her slim bare shoulders and small, firm breasts, her closed eyelids, dark with delicate veins, her quiet breathing in the silence of the night.

In the morning, she went back to her own place, declining breakfast.

'But I'll see you later?' I said. 'You must show me the city.'

She hesitated a little. Then she shrugged, as if dismissing a thought. 'I will meet you at noon, at the coffee stall in the market place,' she said, pointing down the street.

I went to look for Dieter, finding him glooming over coffee in the cavernous dining room. He asked no questions about the night before and I said nothing. After we'd eaten, he said something about sight-seeing, and I had to explain that I'd made my own arrangements. He didn't seem to mind, but I was aware that my face had reddened.

Jenna was waiting at the market square, a huge paved area lined and quartered with trestles and stalls, most of them empty. There were more people there than I'd seen in the streets, a stolid, slow-moving tide of people, queuing to buy kilos of apples from the stalls, or jars of local honey, cloudy and golden, the one touch of luxury in sight. The loudest noise over the shuffle of feet and the murmur of voices was the cackle of hens, tethered by the leg, waiting for purchasers and sudden death. If there was bargaining, it was subdued, and fell silent when the ever watchful men in black leather coats came by, walking slowly, in pairs, hats pulled low over their eyes.

Jenna bought apples and a tiny jar of honey. The wind, raw and blustery, turned her cheeks a healthy pink. We leaned on the high counter of the coffee stall and warmed our hands on chipped enamel mugs. I noticed how she turned her head away as the men in black walked past;

how they eyed her, and then me, and then walked on.

'You don't like them, then?' I said. I suppose it was a foolish question. She bit her lip and looked round. The stall-holder was busy; there was no one near us. She shook her head. I had to lean towards her to catch her words.

'I hate them — hate them,' she said.

We went back to the hotel. Dieter was nowhere to be seen. All the bleak afternoon that slowly darkened towards evening, we made love, lying on the hard bed in the big bare room. And somehow, Jenna turned the bleakness to warmth; somehow I felt we were held in a fragile, enchanted bubble, protected from the outside world by her sweetness and generosity. It was as if she had saved all her warmth, her gentleness, her passion, for these intimate moments, when I felt she was giving me all she had to offer — more than I'd known any woman could offer. Right or wrong, I knew that day that I was in love with Jenna, and I could swear that she -

Later, we lay and talked. Quietly, in case Dieter was in his room next door; confidentially, because there was so little time, and we each wanted — I know we did — to give the other as much as we could of ourselves, our histories, our lives. I told her about my schooldays, my parents; I told her about Gwen and the baby and I told her about my job. I told her about our visit to Suceava, about Dieter's discovery and how we'd cheated the Russians. I knew she'd approve of that. I told her how I'd seen the forests where the wolves howled. And in exchange, she told me about her work; her determination to succeed, to teach at the University, perhaps; about how her parents had disappeared, one day.

'It was a — a purge,' she said. Her voice was matter-of-fact. I asked no questions.

She would not stay to eat with us. 'Dieter will be angry with you,' she said. She dressed and neatly tidied up the bed. She stood by the door, adjusting the red beret. 'I go now,' she said.

'May I see you tomorrow?' I asked. She bit her lip and frowned, then shrugged, as if shaking off an unpleasant thought.

'The same place, then,' she said. 'At noon.'

The hotel had never seemed so empty, so impersonal.

Next day, our last day, I waited at the market place. She didn't turn up. I stayed half the afternoon, slowly freezing to the spot, or stamping up and down. I had no idea where to begin looking for her, no idea where her apartment might be, no idea what might have prevented her from coming. The men in black passed and re-passed me, the hens cackled, the quiet crowds went about their business, but no red beret bobbed amongst them, and, in the late afternoon, I went back to the hotel in the gathering dark, hoping for a message.

There was none and the receptionist was more than usually surly. I went upstairs, to find Dieter's door standing open, and all his possessions strewn about the room.

I ran downstairs and tried to talk to the receptionist, but she couldn't or wouldn't understand.

'The Manager!' I shouted. She shrugged and turned away. 'The Manager! Damn you, woman, I want to talk to the Manager!'

When at last he came, he was small and dark and looked at me with suspicious eyes under black eyebrows.

'Your friend has left, Sir,' he said.

'Left? How can he have left? We have a flight tomorrow – '

He shrugged. 'Perhaps,' he said very deliberately, 'perhaps he is gone to stay with friends.' His eyes went beyond me to where a man in black stood nonchalantly on the other side of the street, studying the posters outside a cinema.

I gaped at him. 'You mean – ?' He turned away from me and went across to the receptionist.

'Have the account ready for this English gentleman,' he said. 'He will be leaving early in the morning.' He bowed, dismissing me.

I went back to my room and sat on the bed, trying to make sense of it. What the hell could they want with Dieter? What was there suspicious about dull, family man Dieter, with his seven languages and his boring, unadventurous caution? I should go to the Consulate, I should ring the Company, I should ring Dieter's wife... In the end, I settled for ringing the Consulate, where they were polite but not very helpful and clearly knew more than I did.

'Well, you know – ' said the very English voice at the end of the line, 'there's really not very much we can do. It's very awkward, very awkward indeed. He should have taken more care. These people are very touchy, very touchy, you know.'

There was nothing I could do. The damage was done.

No-one stopped me leaving the hotel in the morning. I paid the bill and picked up my case and walked out into the cold grey dawn. A taxi was waiting. We passed the market place, deserted at this time of day, and made for the airport. There was no problem, no hitch. Except that I kept looking round, expecting Dieter to arrive, perhaps under escort, but surely they'd send him off on the flight we'd booked, surely he wouldn't be kept back. But he didn't appear.

Just as the flight was called, I saw Jenna. She was headed in my direction. I stood up. Her red beret threaded its way through the crowd, her patent leather feet tapped a sharp pattern on the tiled floor. I couldn't speak. She walked straight past me towards the door marked Police in half a dozen languages, without once looking at me, until she reached it. Then she turned, and her eyes met mine, just for a second, before a black leather arm held the door open, and she was gone.

Then I was on the plane, with an empty seat beside me.

The Chalk Face

Valerie Clarke

The woman sipped her solid mug of dark, steaming tea as she stared through the gaps between the sludge-green letters painted on the window. Thick, brown drips fell from the mug and hit the piece of paper on the table, smudging the deep, blue ink with wet, frilled-edged circles, mingling blue and brown in tiny puddles. The useless words were diluted, illegible. It didn't matter. He wasn't there anyway. Gone. Moved on. No-one knew where.

She took a photograph from her handbag, cradling it gently, as if holding an injured bird, tracing the outline of the face with a mothering finger. He stood solidly, smiling back, confident and hopeful as only the young are.

Her face clouded with sadness as she thought of her empty home. His room was still untouched, waiting for his return. His vibrant paintings still shouted their messages down from the walls: No More Wars; Save the Rain Forests. His half-finished sketches scattered around on his desk. She'd never forgive herself for her angry words.

'Alright if I sit 'ere, love?'

Brenda looked up into the eyes of an old woman, whose head was covered by a grim fur hat, held in place by a long woollen scarf tied under her chin. Both headgear and wearer had seen better days.

'No. I mean yes,' she said. 'No one's sitting there.' She pulled her handbag towards her, protecting her space. She had always been good at putting up barriers.

The old woman's cup rattled precariously, spilling tea into the saucer as she sat down heavily.

'It's always packed here on a dinner-time,' she said, arranging her bags around her legs.

'Oh,' said Brenda, and then, feeling something more was needed, 'I've never been in here before.'

The weary woman stirred a third spoonful of sugar into her cup, spilling more tea into the already full saucer. The clatter of the kitchen activities filled the space between them as Brenda picked up the papers from the table. She had two more addresses to try.

'You looking for a flat or something?'

Brenda looked startled at the woman's boldness.

The woman's leather-skinned face cracked into a laugh, exposing a few broken, brown stained teeth.

'Sorry, but at my age, love, I've no time for wasting on pleasantries.' She poked a finger at the papers in Brenda's hand. 'I saw your addresses, thought you might be flat hunting. Only I know of a place at the back of me, there's a flat going there.'

'Oh, I see.' Brenda's frown lifted. 'No, I'm not looking for a flat.' She hesitated then quickly prised the photograph from between the papers in her hand. 'Actually, I'm looking for my son. This is him. I don't suppose you've seen him, have you? His name's Robert. He's only fifteen.' She thrust the photograph into the woman's rheumatoid hand.

'No, sorry, love.' Her head shook sadly. 'How long's he been gone?'

'Nearly five weeks now.' Brenda bent her head as she stood up and began pushing her things into her neat handbag. Her trembling hands were suddenly covered with the rough, red-worked hands of the old woman. The grip was tight like a clamp, but tenderness passed between the two strangers.

'I hope you find him, love.'

Brenda looked into the woman's cloudy eyes, nodded quickly then pulled away and pushed her way out through the doors onto the busy street.

In the dusty shop doorways, those scorned citizens with no hope or home were taking their places. A withered woman muttered to herself as she pulled in her prized possessions around her, holding tightly to her filthy blanket. Her wild eyes glared at her unwelcome neighbour. Her rival had unrolled his greasy sleeping bag from its frayed string restraint onto a cardboard mat and was sitting behind a strategically placed bowl in view of the passing crowd. A crudely written sign hung around his neck like an albatross. Here, as in many other cities, they waited.

On the corner of the pedestrianised retailers' paradise, a

young man was hunched over the cold grey paving stones. He shifted his position to ease his aching muscles, flexing the multi-coloured fingers of his right hand. He rubbed the pavement with the side of his little finger, blending the shading around the cheek of the woman's face he had created. The pavement was a cruel canvas. He winced with pain as he caught the raw grazed skin on rough stone. As he sucked his finger he scrutinised the face on the pavement. A shroud of black loneliness tried to wrap itself around his body, squeezing until his bones ached. The emptiness in his stomach was only exacerbated by his meagre meals.

The hollow-eyed portrait aroused the sympathy of a passer-by and the young man nodded his head in recognition as a coin dropped into his upturned hat.

He sat back and stretched out his legs, slapping his hands on his torn jeans, then ran his fingers through his thick fair hair, streaking it with fine chalk dust.

The people in the Friday afternoon shopping crowd glanced at his work and hurried on. Did they appreciate the talent of the youth? Probably not. A passing thought, no more.

He glanced into his woollen hat at the few coins cradled in their shabby nest, huddling together for company. He would give it another hour or so, perhaps catch the commuters as they carried home their Friday night generosity. Weekend ahead. Funtime. Out on the town. Their cheerfulness at the freedom from the office routine may loosen their grip on their cash.

'Evening News, get your final!' the paper seller bellowed out the call from a little way down the street. He stamped his feet for warmth.

Robert's finger joints were too stiff with cold to hold a chalk anymore. He blew into his cupped hands.

'Here, Sandra,' a girl called to her friend who was buying a paper. 'Get this, it looks just like you.'

Her friend clip-clopped over, folding her paper into her bag on the way. The girl was pointing at the portrait. She nudged her friend with her elbow.

'Give over, I'm not that old and her mouth's too big. It's nothing like me!' Sandra said indignantly, but dropped a coin into the hat anyway and they hurried off together, sharing their laughter.

The young artist opened a tin box and began to collect his chalks, tossing them haphazardly inside.

'Not much cobalt left,' he said to himself, as he rolled the stub of chalk between finger and thumb.

He shot a look at the money in the hat and sighed as he thought of the home he had left and of his desk drawers crammed full of paints, pastels, charcoal and boards. Everything he needed, just sitting there. Idle, neglected, with no opportunity to give life to his ideas.

He snapped the lid of the box shut. It had been a stupid argument anyway. Lots of things said in the heat of the moment. And now pride kept him from going back.

'On your way now are yer?' The newspaper seller was rubbing his hands together and blowing his breath through his grubby fingerless gloves.

Robert slung his rucksack over his shoulder.

'Yeh, I'm off,' he said. He tipped the coins into the palm of his hand and pushed them around with his finger. He knew he couldn't go on like this. Pocketing the money he walked slowly, with rounded shoulders, into the unfeeling body of the crowd.

Brenda tried hard to hold back her tears of frustration as she walked back towards the station. She came to a litter bin and took the crumpled pieces of paper from her pocket. One by one she ripped up the addresses and scattered them on top of the mountain of cans and burger boxes already overflowing onto the pavement.

She glanced at the town hall clock and hurried on, anxious to catch her train.

'Final, get your final!'

Fumbling in her bag to find some change, she headed towards the newstand.

She stopped. Rigid. Frozen as ice. Her heart leapt and flew at her ribs, beating like a trapped bird desperate for escape. Hot blood rushed round her head, hammering against her skull, surging through her ears, the force of it violently thundering above the crushing of the crowd. She felt weak as her limbs melted and she looked down straight into her own eyes.

The hollow-eyed chalk face on the pavement stared, unmoved, back at its original.

She frantically searched the faces of the crowd, running up and down the street, bringing a startled young man with fair hair spinning round by a desperate pull on his arm. She mumbled her apology and rushed away, darting in and out of the doorways, crying out her son's name, ignoring the hostile stares of the onlookers. She ran to the newspaper seller, shouting, 'Where's the boy gone?'

'Eh?'

'The boy,' she repeated, 'the boy who did the picture,' pointing to the portrait as she took out her purse and thrust a note into his cold hand.

He looked at her panic-stricken face with a puzzled expression, then relaxed. 'Oh, him, I'm sorry, love, he left a while back.' He hesitated as he turned the note over between his cracked fingers, then offered it back to her.

'Where's he gone?' she screamed, pushing the money back towards him.

'I don't know where he goes, he just goes home I 'spect.' He shrugged his shoulders as he carefully folded the note and tucked it into the cuff of his glove.

She swayed and leant on his newstand for support.

'Here, are you alright, love?' His old eyes looked with concern as her tears began to fall, dropping onto the stack of newspapers. The thick black headline shouting Rail Strike Chaos was quietened by a salty stain.

'Why don't you come back tomorrow?'

She heard the soft words through the pounding in her ears.

'He's usually here of a Saturday. More people, you see. Spenders. Them as have a bit to throw around.' He patted her arm gently and then she was gone. He was left shaking his head, watching her tailored raincoat flapping after her as she was swallowed by the crowd.

She tugged the price tag off the sleeping bag as she spread it out in the corner of the doorway. The sky was black above the tall buildings and she shivered. Strange noises drifted towards her on the night air as she pulled her coat around her, hunching up her knees inside the padded cocoon. The moulding on the door behind her was digging into her back like bony knuckles and she squirmed to try to get more comfortable.

For a fleeting moment she wished she had given in to her first thought of going to a hotel, but she wouldn't have slept anyway, and now she was so close she needed to stay, for when he returned.

On the pavement the chalk replica of her face still stared out with sorrow at the empty street. It began to rain. Big heavy drops hit the stone flags in front of her. The chalk face was speckled with wet circles, spreading the colours, mingling blues and greens. The rain fell faster, bouncing off the now grotesque, twisted face, each drop creating a tiny jewelled crown as it hit the wet ground.

The light from the windows danced hopefully in the puddles as she settled down to wait for tomorrow.

Size Twelve

Ailsa Cox

I forgot about the rain. Rain's invisible. You can sit by a window year after year without ever noticing weather. But now I'm on the outside, I can see for myself. Wouldn't you know, it's flipping wet! Today of all days.

'Come on Marje,' says my young lady. 'You'll have to face the weather, if you're going to live at home.'

By home, she means the outside. Sometimes they call it the community, or sometimes your own place, or in a flat. But I'm already in a home; I live inside the hospital.

Something happened to me, a long time ago. I haven't been myself. I used to go on outings quite a lot, at one time. Running down the beach in my plastic mac, wet hair sticking to my cheeks. Water trickling down my collar. Proper bank holiday weather! What you put on these butties, our Marje?

Butties. I used to make them.

'Is it Thursday? I can't go. I'll miss my therapy.'

'You've had thirty years for therapy. Come on now, don't stand there. Come under my umbrella.'

When I take her arm – because she's nice, she lets me – I can breathe all the sweet air inside her. Her face lights up with the colours of the brolly.

'I don't think I'll bother. Not if it's raining. I've been out before, Miss. I'm not so well today.'

'Don't you call me Miss,' she warns.

'We had a picnic in the park, with chocolate cake. The other teacher took us.'

'That was me. And I'm not a teacher. You know that. You remember my name, don't you, Marje?'

'You don't look like a teacher. Teachers don't wear slacks. Sarah.'

'Thanks Marje.'

She doesn't shout like a teacher either. And she can't be a nurse, because she's not in uniform. So what is she? Am I allowed to ask?

'Come on, we'll miss the bus. Have you brought your list with you?'

My wet sandals slap against my feet. Silly sausage, wearing sandals on a day like this! I must've thought I was going to Blackpool. Or Rhyl. Or Southport. I remember Southport, once.

'Today isn't like any other,' my young lady tells me. 'Today's specially for you. How long is it since you've been into Manchester? How long since you bought clothes for yourself? No more fishing in the laundry bag for you. No more baggy drawers and odd socks. From now on, you decide what to wear.'

'I shall be out of style. You're with-it. You look nice. I should try a pair of slacks. Where did you get yours?'

Some funny foreign name. My young lady, Sarah, she wears her hair just like Brigitte Bardot. I wish I could comb that long blonde hair. But I've got to hold on to my purse. I never had so much money before. Never had anything to spend my money on. Only chocolates off the trolley.

A great metal elephant charging towards us — a bus, a real bus! It stops just as I think it's going to mount the pavement and attack us.

'Two sixty-fives please.' Does that squeaky voice belong to me?

'Upstairs or down, Marje?'

I've been practising for this. But real life is bigger, different, it goes altogether faster.

'Upstairs or down?'

'I don't know. What do you think?'

My palms smell of the fancy coins. Thirteen bob's sixty-five pee now, except it isn't really, because everything's gone up.

'Am I allowed upstairs?'

'You do what you like!'

That's right. I'm not going to be scared, even if the bus is going too fast. Now I'm going to make a conversation.

'Got a boyfriend, then?'

'No-one special,' she says.

From the upstairs, the streets are spread around like cinerama.

'I bet you got loads of chaps. I bet you go dancing. Rock

and roll!'

The bus swings round the corners, rock and a-rolling, and big-dippering. Branches of trees scrape the windows. When we stop under a bridge, I can tell the sound of trains overhead, most probably the diesel engines.

'Let's check this list once more, shall we?'

Pay attention, Marje. You're being spoken to.

'Seven pairs of knickers, triple pack of tights. You'll need to keep replacing tights, of course, as they get snagged. But everything else should last you, if we spend our money sensibly. Sensibly! Sorry, Marje, if I sound just like your mother, when I know I'm young enough to be your child! It's just, when you're managing on the social, you'll really have to learn to make things stretch. But we've talked about that, haven't we?'

'I've dropped behind. There was no such thing as tights before I was ill. Stockings and suspenders – digging right in you. You had to hold your breath and the draught went right up. I shall have to follow the fashions. Where's all the shops gone? There used to be shops running all the way to town. I'm right, aren't I? I'm not mixed up? Where's Rosselli's ice cream parlour?'

Everywhere looks out of sorts. I can see tall, skinny buildings, standing sentry, either side of the main road. I can see boarded-up churches, and factories with their windows broken. There are one or two trees, tangled up with plastic bags. But the first thing that you notice is all the empty spaces.

'Beg your pardon. I'm mistaken. I never lived round here.'

Think of something else.

'Never been here before.'

Something else.

'I say, is that what they're wearing these days – see the way she's dressed? Is that the rage – green hair?'

'Shush, Marje! Don't point!'

'What do you call that stuff on her legs? Is it snakeskin?'

She's just like those funny reptiles in the zoo. I used to go to the zoo. And next to her, another sight to be seen, a woman all wrapped in sheeting, like Mary in the stable.

'Iranian,' my young lady whispers.

Iranian. Sounds like a green-eyed monster. Iranian. Perhaps the space films have come true. I should've spent my pocket money on newspapers, instead of buying all those toffees.

'Marjorie, try not to stare. People don't like it. We're not on the ward now.'

Now I can look through the window and see where I really am. The old clock towers are still standing, and the town hall and the skyscrapers, all of them pointing upwards, like rockets on alert. I can't breathe, I'm so excited.

Deep breath! Wiggle into that panty girdle! My new dress slips over my head. When I see myself in the mirror, I know tonight's going to be lucky. Derek's going to be there, I just know he will. When I walk into the Ritz, he'll turn round instinctively. His eyes will be drawn towards the girl in red. Hasn't he seen her somewhere before? Can this be – Marjorie?

The dress hangs stiffly at the waist, like paper wrapped around a bouquet. I spent hours backcombing and lacquering. Everything's just right. And then – and then.

Trust you, Marje! Every time I put new stockings on, I have to ladder them. I start pulling through the stuff in the drawer, trying to untangle nearly-new from mended. Trust you, Marje, to keep your drawer a mess! The bus is coming round the corner. I can see it through my window. Now I'll have to run.

I can't. I'm stuck – stuck – like dreams when you're running through sand. It's the high heels. Take them off, quick! My feet hurt as I go. My hairdo's dropping loose. The lads on the top deck are laughing. Dirty brutes. Juvenile delinquents. But there's Derek, what's he doing, like a monkey at the window?

He noticed me alright. Not that it really matters. We still had some fun, me and the girls.

'Do you go to the Ritz, Miss – Sarah? I love to go dancing. I like the pictures too, when you've got someone with you.' Meet you there at half-past. The Odeon, the Empire and the Gaumont. Is my slip showing? Are my stockings straight? 'I bet you look nice in a frock. Can we go to Boots, try on some scent?'

'If we have time.' She smiles. 'I'll bring in some makeup, next time I'm on the ward.'

'Lets go to Woolworth's.'

Backs of our hands, smeared pink and blue. Keep away from the counter, girls, if you're not buying! We're hanging round the mirror in the toilets, spitting in mascara, drawing darker eyebrows, fiddling with our hair. Are my roots showing, Marje?

'Woolworth's shut,' says Sarah.

'What you mean? Is it Wednesday? What you bring me for, on half-day closing?'

'Marje, they don't have half-day closing now, not in the city centre. What I mean is, Woolworth's closed down. It's shut. It's gone. There's lots of new shops now. Time to get off! We're there. You'll soon see for yourself.'

But what is there to see? Where are we? It's a long drop from the bus, but I'm still trying. My young lady holds the brolly like a shield in front of us and we charge outwards, forwards, into the middle of whatever it is, the outside, the city centre, the community.

'Be careful!' Didn't they teach her? Look right, look left, look right again. And if it's safe to cross – 'Oh be careful! Wait!' But she says, don't worry, you'll soon get used to traffic.

I want to sit down. But the benches are all full of tramps. I can see a boy playing a tin whistle. There's a label round his neck and it says I AM HUNGRY. I can't see Lewis's. Where's Lewis's? Where's Market St.? I know it must be here. Manchester's like that jigsaw puzzle in the dayroom. All the pieces must belong somewhere.

'Now then, where's our list... British Home Stores -

Littlewood's – Marks and Spencer – C.& A. – are you listening, Marje? Where shall we go first? Don't be afraid.'

Market St. – Corporation St. – Cross St. – Piccadilly – Victoria – Albert Square – the names keep running through my head. Kardomah – Blackfriars Bridge – just like jigsaw pieces, waiting to be picked up again.

'Don't worry, I've got you. You won't be run over. Watch the green man, Marje, just like I showed you.'

I want to buy a present.

Used to buy a lot of presents. Always hot in Lewis's at

Christmas. Can't ever find my way out. Is that something burning? People crowding round the exits. Lifts aren't working. Everyone pretending nothing wrong. Play along with them, Marje, don't let on you know. Run right down, soon as you find the stairs, all the way down the iron bannisters, but where is the way out, can't ever find it, not at Christmas time, so hot and crowded...

'You can relax now, Marje. We're on a pedestrian precinct. No cars allowed.'

'But the people're going too fast. They've all got prams and trolleys...' I never can find the way out.

I make myself stand still for a minute, while I think quietly to myself.

A present. Hot and crowded.

'Where's that shop you got your slacks from?'

'Sorry, Marje, it's a bit expensive. And to be honest, I don't think it's quite your style.'

The hair swings over her face. Why won't she tell me why I can't go to Woolworth's?

'I just want to have a look.'

'Okay, we're going past there anyway.'

I have to look down, because the buildings knock me dizzy. The street's like a fairground, all tangled up with wheels and heels and umbrella spokes. Watch your feet. Watch your eyes. The rain keeps on spitting. THE WEATHER TODAY – TWO WEEKS IN BARBADOS – SPECIAL OFFER. They shouldn't put those moving lights up there. I fall over legs every time I try to read them.

Elvis – James Dean – Marilyn. So they're still going then. I give two shillings to the boy chalking faces on the pavements. But the rain'll wash the pictures clean away. Unless they have a special chalk. They might do nowadays. And banjo players too! And a young man with a violin and someone selling squashy balloons with pictures of Mickey Mouse.

'Marje, this is the shop.'

No wonder my young lady won't talk about her boyfriend. She's got some fancy man to buy expensive clothes. All of a sudden, the money in my purse, it feels like nothing.

But I did want to buy her a thank you present.

Inside the new shopping centre, everything goes still. You could be back on the ward. Not that it's what you call quiet. Gangs of lads are running up the moving staircase. Children keep skidding across the shiny tiles. Songbirds are twittering in cages and you can hear water splashing from somewhere. Yet every sound's like the noise inside a seashell. It is exactly like the ward, white and airless, like the inside of a fridge. None of the shops have got names I remember. Miss this and Man that and other mysterious names. Next what? What Next? Perhaps part of the sign has dropped off.

Behind the glass, the dummies are stark naked. The women have got nipples and the men have got pouches underneath. Most realistic. They have deep, slanting eyes like Jean Simmons.

'Right,' says my young lady. 'Let's get down to business. Have you decided which shop to try first? How about British Home Stores?'

'I want to go in here.' Inside, the shop's enormous. Racks and racks of frocks, yet they all look just the same.

'What about this one? This is lovely. It'd suit you.'

Besides, I don't want a frock, not really. I want a pair of slacks like my young lady's, in just that shade of beige.

'Light colours show the dirt, Marje. Listen. Don't you think, to be honest, Marje... This one's just your style.'

And aren't I lucky? They've got them in Size 12.

No proper cubicles – everyone together in a big changing room, strangers undressing side-by-side. You can smell sweat. Not like under the nurse's arm when she reaches over the lightswitch. This smell's heavy with the outdoors. A thick smell, like petrol.

I am not a Size 12.

I can't even pull the trousers up over my knees.

I am not Size 12.

Times have changed. You don't have private cubicles these days. Everyone can see you. But at least there aren't assistants hanging around, calling you Madam.

'They make these sizes small. I'll have to go into a Size 14.'

'To be quite honest,' she says, this skinny little girl with hair in her eyes, this Sarah with her fancy man, 'frankly,

Marjorie, I don't think a fourteen'll do it.'

'Get off! I've never been more than a Size 12 before.'

She's got a point, this Sarah. I can't drag the next pair much further than my thighs. I'm not a Size 14.

'I'll get a sixteen for you.'

'I'm not a sixteen! How can I be? I've always had a nice figure! Size 16!'

'Marjorie,' she calls gently, in her bad news voice, 'Marjorie, you've been in hospital a long time. You aren't a young woman any more. You've had no exercise. And you know what hospital food's like. You're bound to have put on a little bit of weight. That's why I don't really think this kind of shop suits you.'

'But I've still got my figure. I couldn't lose my figure, I'd notice. I'd start dieting.'

'Marjorie, have you looked at yourself recently?'

Why should I? I don't get visitors. At one time, I used to powder my face. 'Come on,' the nurses said, 'smarten yourself up, it's that dishy Doctor Dennis!' He couldn't remember my name without looking at his notes.

The nurses were playing a joke. What does it matter what you look like in the bin?

'Marjorie.'

The changing room's full of mirrors. We're standing right in the middle of a big kaleidoscope of round behinds, bra straps and dangling busts. None of these bodies belong to film stars. They're nothing like the dummies in the window. But neither are they anything like mine.

When I do as I'm told – when I look straight at myself – all I can find is a fat old woman. An old bag. A fat cow. A big sack of spuds. Now I've broken my zip, hurrying to get out.

'Oh! I'm a big clumsy fool!' Big bum. Droopy tits. Barmpot. You must be mental.

'It doesn't matter. Your hospital clothes aren't even worth another wash.'

Is that my face in the mirror, red and slack? Why, when I washed my hair, did I never see the colour going from it? No-one's ever going to stroke my hair.

'Don't be upset. Everyone matures. You just have to choose the right style. It doesn't mean you have to dress dowdily.'

'Do they have any shops for fat people?'

'Perhaps,' she says slowly, 'it might be an idea to try the oversize shops. They do some very nice things nowadays. But there's the chainstores as well. You aren't that overweight. You aren't a freak, Marjorie.'

Yes I am. To myself I am. Nothing in the big stores touches me. We're obliged to go somewhere that caters for the fuller figure. The dummies in the window aren't fat. The clothes hang loose on their super slinky figures like decorators' sheets.

'These are lovely,' says the little girl with me. 'Look! This colour suits you. You'll look so sophisticated!'

I have to try, for her sake, to show an interest. She found me a flat. She's even going to help with decorating. But now it doesn't matter what I wear. I'm much too fat.

If we'd gone to Woolworth's, I could've bought a little present. I could've proved I wasn't an ungrateful, fat old woman.

Yes, I keep on saying, very nice. Two of those. That's right. Sometimes I pick something up, just to show willing.

My young lady buys two coffees. It comes to over a pound. She does not take sugar. I take three. She's talking to me from far away, on the other side of the table. She's asking me about the flat, what colour for the kitchen? She can get a television free, but there's the license. Do you want a TV, Marje?

A picture's playing in my head. A lazy fat old woman, watching TV in a tent dress.

Is my slip showing, Marje? Where you going Saturday? Who you going with this time? You're not! He keeps French letters in his pocket. He does, honestly! What you wearing, Marje? What colour lipstick do they call that?

He'll gaze into your eyes and say, 'Why, you're beautiful...' He leans forward and he takes your hand.

Sarah said something.

'Are you alright, Marje?' She's a lovely-looking girl, in her cream-coloured slacks. She holds my hand and asks me, 'Are you tired?'

I can't help myself. I have to speak.

'I don't understand! What happened to me? I don't feel old; inside myself, I'm not fat. Can't you see? It's just the outside that's altered. I'm Marjorie! It's me!'

Someone's listening, a woman at the next table. Her tight, watchful eyes are trapped beneath the skin. I've never seen a woman so wrinkled. But she isn't as ugly as me.

'Do you know what happened?' I ask her. 'Do you understand?'

The woman pretends not to hear.

'Somebody ought to explain.'

My young lady's gone quiet. She just looks at me and smiles sadly, and pulls her coat back on. Time to go home. Fish finger time. We always have fish fingers on a Thursday.

Getting It

Helen Smith

I have to talk myself into the day. Hey, it's morning. Hey, it's good to be alive. I kid myself along.

My name is Janet Lowell, I am thirty-eight years old. It's a really bad day if I need to remind myself.

Just think. There's honey for breakfast and a banana. A tin of Katkins to be opened for Hercules. With luck, by this time, I've found my slippers and I'm shuffling off to the bathroom.

Otherwise I'm curled up inside the duvet, mad, bad and dangerous to know, re-opening every wound they ever inflicted on me, with no chance of getting up until the 8.30 panic strikes. The world news is infiltrating the pillow on my head, another missile on target for a blanket hit.

* * *

'Morning, Hercy.'

The banana has a mottled brown skin. The honey has gone to crystals in the bottom of the jar.

Hercules wolfs down his Katkins and struts out through the cat flap.

'Morning Janet, thanks for the Katkins, Janet, have a nice day and see you later, Janet,' I say on Hercules' behalf. Someone has to keep up the niceties of everyday conversation.

Off down the road. Look at the gardens, a new For Sale board at the end. Round the corner and the avenue of trees. Bare, tall, powerful, some days I manage to stir some feeling on their behalf.

The thing I try not to think about, the thing I try not to think about on my way to work, is hard to avoid. Think about work at the end of this walk and a deep gloom settles down over the trees. If it was a proper library with dusty books and withered women, no talking, no eating and no toilets, I could be withered and spend the whole day shushing and stamping. I could handle that.

Instead, around the corner is the cultural centre, community facility. We deal in information, storing it, retrieving it, and even handing it over. I don't get to read the books, which is what I went into the job for.

'It must be lovely working with people,' says Julie. Huh.

'You get to meet all sorts in the library,' she goes on. Double huh.

'Like that Paula, you liked her,' says Julie.

She never knows when to stop. I have a rule not to contradict everything she says. Otherwise it'd look as if I was disagreeable for the sake of it and, after all, Julie is only motivated by niceness. She is also my last, my only friend. People took my side to begin with, but I'm so disagreeable they disappeared. I'd just rather be disagreeable than depressed.

So I restrict myself to politely mentioning that I merely took an interest in Paula's welfare.

'You fancied her.'

'Shut it, Julie.'

Now, of course, Julie is hurt.

I make it up to her by telling her the news I've been hugging to myself.

'Actually, Julie, she popped into the library today. Yes, Paula. After all this time.'

I did, of course. Fancy Paula. Not straight away, because she wasn't my type. At first all I saw was a young girl, a trainee based in the library. Dressed the way sixteen year olds dress, but with thick chestnut hair that rioted just above her shoulders. I did notice her hair.

Marvin moaned about her all the time. She got to work late, she did nothing but drink coffee, she didn't know her alphabet. 'Girls these days,' became his catchphrase.

I'd be making a dash for the staff room, and there she'd be, drinking coffee with her feet up. She'd make coffee for everyone and ask interested questions and soon knew more about everyone's home life than the rest of us put together. We all liked her. Marvin was the only one who took the YTS even half seriously.

She had quite a way with her. She was friendly and had a lot of confidence for a kid. She was dark with almond-shaped brown eyes and by the time I was thinking about her body I realised I found her very sexy indeed.

'I wish I could work with you, Miss Lowell,' she said. 'Working with Marvin's great, but the way you talk about your work makes it sound really interesting.'

I was flattered, although it was perfectly obvious that she was flattering me. That's when it started, knowing that she was flirting.

I told Julie what Paula said about Marvin.

'He's always looking at my legs. Honestly. It makes me self-conscious, my calves are really fat.' She was holding out her legs for me to judge.

'What's wrong with them?' I said.

'I like thin legs,' she said, 'I ought to lose weight.'

'What on earth for?' I said coolly.

And she came back with, 'what do you think of them?'

'Girls these days,' said Julie.

It was nice at first, feeling sexy and alert. Alive and glad to be. Julie noticed my new clothes. 'What's up with you?' she said.

Not much was up with me, except that I lingered a little longer in the staff room than I had done before, drank a little more coffee. That was all the obvious signs. But every other moment I was fitting in thoughts of Paula. Waiting for a phone call to connect, I'd be following my daydreams down lustful alleys, where a kid of sixteen was making me feel good.

It lasted until I overheard her talking to Marvin about me.

I'd gone to collect an exhibition from the City Art Gallery. There were going to be boxes of stuff to load into the van and, although I could have managed on my own, I asked Marvin to lend me Paula.

That was fine with Marvin, and Paula seemed pleased. In fact, she jumped at the chance. It's crazy, but walking to the van, I felt nervous.

We got to town. Paula made a comment on the way, about hands looking nice on driving wheels, which I took personally, and which turned me half to jelly. We loaded up and, when we were nearly ready to go, she cleared her throat and asked me a favour. Would I mind if she popped off, just for five minutes, to see her Mum who worked round the corner?

I said fine, and sat back in the seat to enjoy watching her walk away from me. Here was some free time made for dreaming in.

'She'll come back around that corner,' I thought, 'and walk towards me. Hair swinging around her face.'

Paula would come to the van door and swing herself in, her eyes wide and warm. She would turn to face me and her hand would move across, and her face would come closer and closer until she was... her face so close... until her mouth was on mine, kissing me.

I opened my eyes fast at that point. I could hardly breathe. I could feel her touch on my skin. Here, above my elbow, the fantasy fingers had closed on my arm.

Her fingers on my arm. She would slide the van door open and climb into her seat. Then she would look at me, look at me long and hard and she would touch my arm, and lean forward, and then, oh yes, the kiss.

Rewind back to the kiss. Her mouth soft and warm. Warm, and her lips wanting me, her lips. I practically came at this point. I couldn't breathe and I couldn't swallow.

Just then Paula came swinging round the corner. Swung up to the door and yanked it open and crashed it shut. Sat staring out through the windscreen.

'Aren't we going then?' she said, and I mumbled something and scrunched the gears and we went back to work.

I made a little conversation. She didn't reply, just stared out the window.

It didn't hit me until later, what an absolute fool I was. Head over heels for a kid of sixteen. It wasn't just that she was sixteen, and that I'd always prided myself that I'd only want an equal relationship. It was that I'd been mooning around full of feelings and wantings and needings. Not my usual horrible self at all.

* * *

So, here she is in the library.

'Hello, Miss Lowell,' she says, softer, not as cheeky as

she used to be. Here she is, sitting in the rest room, her beautiful hair permed stiff into tight curls, and rocking the buggy. Sitting in the buggy is a solemn child staring at me out of brown almond-shaped eyes.

'Aren't you a beautiful baby,' I say. You can say things to babies you can't say to their mothers. 'Aren't you gorgeous.' There's a silence.

'And what about you, Paula? What are you up to now?'

'Not a lot,' she says. 'Not much chance, really.' She looks at the baby. It's not a doting look, more the look of someone who hasn't had her feet up in the last five months.

'Put your feet up,' I tell her. 'I'll make some coffee.'

She smiles at me.

'I haven't had my feet up since I was here,' she says, pointing her toes and looking critically at her legs. 'Hey, Miss Lowell, how's Hercules?' Her voice sounds young again.

'He's fine. He's turning into quite a hunter. Left me two worms on the kitchen floor, yesterday.' She laughs.

'And I've got a baby,' she says, not laughing any more.

'I didn't want her, you know,' she says. 'I wasn't after a baby. Honest, I don't know how it happens that you want one thing and get another.'

'What did you want, Paula?'

'I wanted excitement. I wanted sex too, but I thought there'd be more to it. Do you know what I mean, Miss Lowell?'

'Mmm,' I admit.

'It's weird, isn't it, because you think excitement would be sex or drugs or stolen cars.'

'They're not exciting then?' I ask her.

'No. I get car sick. My Mum reckons it's the sort of thing you have to go out and look for, and then you end up finding it inside after all.'

I'm thinking, could her Mum tell me how to find the feeling, and she goes on, 'haven't time to look for anything much, with looking after this one. I might go to college. I'm off sex though. Do you like it?'

* * *

'Fancy her saying that to you,' says Julie. 'She must really like you, to come out with things like that.'

'She said the same thing to Marvin five minutes later,' I tell Julie.

'But you don't say things like that to an old stick sort of person,' Julie says.

That was what I'd overheard Paula saying to Marvin that time. After the van and before she stopped coming into work.

'Miss Lowell's not a bad old stick.' Funny, because it made me feel just like one. Very bad, very old, very stickish. Lustful and ashamed.

I've dug out some stuff for Paula about colleges and creches. I suppose she could find what she's after there, like her Mum says.

Where would I find what I'm after?

Julie would answer that question for me by opening her arms and inviting me to walk right in. I've taken to contradicting everything she says, but she doesn't appear to notice.

I don't want Paula any more. I fancy someone else, in an old stickish sort of way.

So that's three of us after something. Julie thinks she knows what she wants. Paula will know what she wants once she gets it. And me? Whatever it is that I want, only one thing's clear. I'm not getting it.

A Fish in the Sky

Pat Winslow

Georgia loved every brick in that city, every stacked car in the scrapped metal yards, every terracotta chimney pot. Some days she would take the tram that rode over the iron bridge strutting the canal. She would gaze out past the fingernail scratch marks that the rain made on the windows and she would look down onto the saw-toothed factory roofs. Mill hands. That was what always came into her mind then. Scores of them twisting and turning, winding, taking off, putting on. And in the breaks, lighting up and stubbing out, scratching noses, straightening out hair, smoothing down nylon stockings, applying make-up. Hands. Scores of them.

When she looked at her own she saw other worlds. Deep gorges cut into hard red rock. Dried up river beds that cracked like eczema under a blazing sun. Today they were veined with semi-precious stones – purple amethysts and chalcedony, blue howlite, black opals, heliotrope, tourmaline. If she cut them they would bleed out of her leaving her skin white and empty. A powdery moonscape of soft ridges. A fragile land that could be blown away like dust. Just like dust.

She looked at the tower blocks, at the bases where the crumpled newspapers and broken milk bottles had gathered. Sixties concrete. The only flower power she'd ever seen were the crushed daisies lying amongst the dog turds. Hard to believe that so much optimism had produced these red and grey obelisks with fading blue panels and dirty washing hanging out of the windows.

She didn't like using the lift. It was like being sealed alive in a metal tomb. Once those doors were closed anything could happen. There was a recess at the back just long enough to accept a coffin. It only went half-way up the wall and she'd often wondered why they hadn't made the lift bigger in the first place. Today there were three young boys larking around in it. She thought of them being trapped in there forever with their spray cans and Doc Martens. What would they eat once they'd got past the packets of crisps and chocolate bars, she wondered. Which one would they cannibalize first? The pale one with the small hands probably. The one who reminded her of a brown mouse she'd once seen scuttling along her skirting board.

Slowly she climbed the stairs, dragging her plastic bags behind her. Walter Hopwood was her favourite block. It was full of different smells and noises. There was a large white family on the fourth floor and they always had the television on. If she'd had a watch she could have set it by them. Good Morning with Anne and Nick, ten-thirty. Neighbours, one-thirty. Home and Away, Blockbusters – one-forty-five, ten past five. They seemed to live on television. Television and cabbage and boiled potatoes, and, once or twice, fish. On the next floor there was a single mother with a son whose voice was breaking. He was forever whining at her and slamming doors. Sometimes she could smell perfume or soapy bath water when she passed them. Other days it was toast or chips.

There was one floor she always paused on though. The combined smells from the three neighbouring flats made her feel so weak that she would have to sit down and rest a while. Fresh coffee, liver and onions, marijuana, incense, curry, bacon and eggs, newly washed sheets, bread. She never knew which smell came from which flat or in what combination, but they were all awash with sunshine and pot plants, she felt sure. On the fourteenth floor it was summer. Permanently.

On the twenty-first it was whatever it was outside. Today it was spring. Georgia waited by the emergency escape till the lift stopped humming. The boys had been going up and down in it all morning and now, for a moment at least, it was silent. Quickly, she took a pair of wire cutters out of one of her bags and cropped the thin chain that was holding the padlock. It slipped silently and she caught it before it fell at her feet.

Delinquent. What a delicious word that seemed. She rolled it over in her mouth like a sherbet lemon, testing its rough edges and feeling the fizz of it explode against her tongue. At sixty-four, Georgia was planning a rooftop escape. The three boys downstairs were merely joyriding in a piss-sticky lift. Up and down, up and down, all day long amongst the empty Coke cans and styrofoam trays. She pushed the metal bar inwards and opened the door. The sun greeted her like a joyous laugh.

She could see everything from up there. The University, MacDonalds, the train station with its tiny signal box at the end, the metal grills on the post office window, the pillar box. Even the dogs running around down below. Everything was in miniature, doll's house proportioned, and she marvelled at the endless possibilities. If she reached down with one of her giant's hands now, she could scoop something up and turn it over in her palms. She could feel the length and weight of it. She could put it somewhere else perhaps. Redesign the whole city if she wanted to.

The traffic lights were no bigger than her fingers. Six lanes of cars roared through them like pulsing blood cells. Stop start go. Stop start go. They were like an irregular heart beat. The city's life supply. Except they were choking it. The tell-tale strangulation marks were everywhere. An entire row of houses had been squashed out only the other day. And a car park existed where the Gaumont cinema had once been.

A bus was getting rid of its passengers, defecating like a squatting dog by the kerb. Georgia held out her hand and encircled one of them with her thumb and forefinger. I could squash you, she was thinking. I could squash you now and no one would ever know who did it. She didn't though. She let him go. An hour ago it had been her down there. She'd been a tiny insect just like him. Strange to think that she was the giant now. The only giant. She looked around her at eye level. No one else was standing on top of the flats. No one else had the imagination. She sat down and began to rummage in one of the plastic bags for her sandwiches. She'd brought a flask of tomato soup, a candle and a blanket, should she decide to stay the night, a bin liner that she could crawl into in case it rained, and her kite.

As Georgia ate she found herself besieged by pigeons

and seagulls. It mystified her how they could spot a crumb of bread from so far away. Looking down to the paved precinct below she could just about make out the afternoon's chip wrappers, but she couldn't see any chips. Perhaps the pigeons had eaten them. She tossed a piece of bread into the air and watched in admiration as a seagull dropped down and caught it mid-flight. They were huge birds. She hadn't realized how big they were until they spread their wings. They looked so tight and compact on the ground. So earthbound somehow. Georgia shuffled forward till she was near the edge and dangled her legs over the side of the building. She was being very daring now, she realized. A couple more shuffles and she'd be over the top and falling to her death. It thrilled her to think she was this close to her own mortality. That she had that choice if she wanted to make it. She continued eating her sandwiches and taking small sips from the cup of hot soup by her side. Suicide should never be contemplated on an empty stomach, she reflected. It gave an entirely false perspective.

The city was growing softer lately, especially now that the evenings were lighter. Georgia squinted at the skyline. She could see four fat chimneys rising like vases from the factory wastelands. They had stopped smoking and were drinking in the late sun. The rush hour roar had just begun. She didn't hear it at first. It came like a tap dripping, just out of range of her consciousness. But suddenly it was there, below her, stretched out all around her. Cars shrieking, lorries rumbling. The arteries were swollen and pumping hard, bleeding the city dry. It was time to fly her kite.

The other two were like dogs. Big hard muscular creatures that barked about their exploits and peed in dark alleyways. They were always sniffing out the exciting things to do. Nicking fags and grabbing handfuls of sweets from the toffee shop when the owner wasn't looking. Setting fire to car tyres and old chair cushions. Sniffing glue. Joe had grown tired of them. They'd been going up and down in the lift all morning. Up down, up down. It had been never-ending. Why don't we do something else, he'd asked. They'd sniggered at him – why don't we do something else? Like what, for fuck's sake? Joe hadn't known. He never knew. They were the dogs. Not him. They'd gone off eventually to have a wank in the stairwell of the empty tower block that was about to be pulled down and now he was alone sitting on a ripped-out car seat watching the yellow coltsfoot waving in the wind.

He bent forward to pick some and stopped when he saw how pale and slight his fingers were. A memory came to him then of when he'd first noticed his shadow. How his father had laughed and picked him up in his great square hands. Joe pushed his angry fists deep into his pockets and sat back in the seat. Spanking hands. Absent hands. His would never grow like that no matter how hard he tried. He looked up at Walter Hopwood turning red in the sinking sun and saw the windows shining like mirrors all down it. It was a platinum evening, almost gold yet still not quite free of that winter whiteness they'd all endured for so long. Someone was flying a kite from the top of the flats. From where he was sitting it looked small and black but every so often it would turn in the wind and the sun would catch it. It was purple then. Large and purple and triumphant. He would be that kite if he could. He would soar above everyone with his arms outstretched and buck and swoop and leap and sway and chase his tail until the sun went down. He would swallow air like it was clear fresh water. He would be a fish in the sky.

Joe stood up, still with his hands in his pockets, and began to walk away. His shadow had grown long whilst he'd been sitting there and now it covered the turf and broken glass with its singular straightness. A pencil pointing the way home. He followed it, never once allowing his eyes to look upwards. The others were waiting for him. They'd bought condoms they said. They were going shagging. When Joe refused to go with them they called him Queer and Poof. He could still hear their voices when he was in the lift. They sounded afraid. As though by going he had somehow left them feeling exposed and vulnerable. He pressed number twenty-one and sat down in the space where the coffins went. Just a taste was all he wanted. The knowledge of what it was like to be up there.

When Georgia started to reel the kite back in she had the unexpected feeling that she was also pulling something else in. The line had become umbilical. The kite was still swaying above her, but it had a bruised look now. It seemed crushed and bloody like an autumn plum. Yet it was spring. And spring made oranges out of things, not plums. She turned towards the sun as if to confirm this but found it sinking behind a row of dirty brown buildings. When she turned back the kite had fallen. It was opposite her, almost on a level with her shoulders. She heard the roof door open behind her and someone step out. The line went slack.

His wail caught her completely by surprise. At first, she thought it was the kite, when it began to plummet into a nose dive down past the top four storeys. But when she saw the open arms and legs spinning after it, when she saw the thin hands and the dull crop of brown hair standing out on the small head, she knew immediately. He was like a mouse that had been picked up by its tail and thrown across a room.

Fascinated, she watched him as he hurtled down towards the ground. It seemed to take forever. Then suddenly he stopped. There was no noise. Nothing to signal his arrival. He just lay there, splayed out on the precinct in the shape of a badly written four. Georgia let the kite go. It fluttered for a moment like an open mouth trying to grasp something. A fish nibbling at the air. She'd always wondered why fishes drowned on dry land. Now as she watched the kite descend to where the boy was lying, it occurred to her that perhaps she'd never know the answer to that question.

The winding reel landed first. It landed right next to him. And as the crowds gathered round and the sirens began to echo across the city, the kite caught a new current of air. It rose and rose above the boy's body, dragging the reel with it. Someone looked up and tried to catch it, but he couldn't quite reach the line. The kite was swimming too fast and too far away. Georgia watched it disappear beyond the park and the trees. It was heading for the ship canal. Flying out to sea.

Biographies

Glenda Brassington

I was born in Coventry in 1965. I studied in Cardiff before moving to Manchester. I am a member of Starstruck Theatre Company and last year they produced my first play *High Rise Society* which toured the North West before going on to the Edinburgh Festival.

Sylvia Christie

Born in Aberdeen sometime in the early cretaceous period, inhabited Stockport for three decades; not yet quite extinct. Teach Creative Writing for WEA and Stockport College; fond of travel, comfort, Discworld novels, food; not fond of wet weather, Christmas, housework, blockbusters. Happy to be back in Commonword/Crocus books.

Valerie Clarke

I share my Flixton house with Matthew and Cadence (son and daughter) Dinky (cat) and Calvin, Hobbes and Cecil (gerbils). My writing is slotted in between being a mother, interviewing for market research companies, Citizen's Advice Bureau work, improving my French and doing up our home. I had a story published by Commonword in *Relative to Me* and have had some success in competitions. I write in the small hours and have many pieces which have been almost finished for a long time. I am writing a children's fantasy at the moment and have many notes and scribblings for a novel which I hope to begin one day before my ink or my brain runs dry.

Ailsa Cox

Size Twelve was inspired by something I read while I was doing typing work for students. Other stories have appeared in various collections, including *The Virago Book of Love and Loss* and Crocus's *Holding Out* anthology. I'm also co-editor, with Elizabeth Baines, of *Metropolitan*, a new fiction magazine. I live in Manchester.

Julie Farrand

I was born in 1959, and grew up in a small village in Hampshire on the top of a hill. I was a solitary, anxious little girl who went for a lot of long walks. Thirteen years ago I moved to Manchester. I was caught by the throat, and the city hasn't let me go since.

José Gent

Thrilled when my first contribution to literature (all sixteen lines of it) was published in *No Earthly Reason?*, fame went to my head when someone asked 'Have you heard about José? She's in A BOOK!' Voluntary work with homeless people taught me a lot and thanks to them I'm in ANOTHER BOOK.

Noel Hannan

I am a 26 year old printer living in Crewe with my wife Helen and dog Bella. My book *Wild Tundra* was a finalist in Commonword's novel competition, and I have recently been commissioned by American publisher Fantaco to script a series of comic books based around the movie *Night of the Living Dead*, to be illustrated by Leeds artist Rik Rawling. Buy them and make us happy!

Julie Lerpiniere

I was born this time around in Scarborough and spent my childhood sailing the high seas. Moved to Manchester in 1981 and now live in the Bury area with 4 pigeons and the ghost of a World War 1 soldier. Work in progress: 2 collections of short stories and a novel.

Fokkina McDonnell

'Dutch-born ex-sailor becomes best-seller writer'. Not quite. I was a secretary and assistant purser before studying psychology. Now I help people change jobs and career. Obscure magazines publish my haiku poetry and *The Visit* is my second story in print, so I am on track for that career change!

Paul Morris

I spent my pubescent years living in the Nottinghamshire borderlands, but left home for London and work. Cities have always attracted me. I was born in Manchester and eventually found my way back there for three years as a self-conscious student. I owe the Civil Service a great deal – without the futile year I spent handing out giros at Great Ancoats Street I never would have taken my pretensions to writing seriously. My creative energies are now sapped by teaching in Oldham.

Valérie Olek

I was born in France in 1965 and grew up in a village near Lyons. I moved to Bolton four years ago and work at the University of Manchester as a secretary. I love writing stories. This one is influenced by the tales of my mother's childhood in North Africa.

Qaisra Shahraz

I am thirty-five years old, married and have three sons. I originally came from Pakistan twenty-three years ago. I studied at the Universities of Manchester and Salford, gaining B.A and M.A Hons degrees respectively. I teach English in a local college. I have been writing for over thirteen years, and have had articles published in *She* magazine, and short stories in different anthologies both in England and in Germany, including *Invitation to Literature, Twentieth Century Writing Women, What Big Eyes You've got, Holding Out* and *Black and Priceless*. Most of my stories deal with themes relating to my own Muslim, Pakistani culture. I have won two prizes for short stories.

Christopher B. Skyrme

Born in 1964. I moved around a lot as a child, living in Hertfordshire, Edinburgh, Birmingham, France, Leicestershire and the Basque Country before settling in Manchester. I have been here now for ten years, during which time I have run a community theatre company, been a teacher at several schools and worked in theatre. Currently I work for It's Queer Up North and The Village Charity. *I would like to dedicate this story to Ian.*

Catriona Smith

I was born and brought up in Nottingham in a family so ripe for rebelling against Morrissey would have wept. In 1987 I fled to Manchester University but found studying Geology no spiritual path but a Berghaus hell. This short story is the first and only I have submitted (smirk smirk) so far. I live in Hulme, write for *The Big Issue* and have never been mugged. Yet.

Helen Smith

I'm 40 this year which will make it a good year to write my first novel. This feels like a difficult project but my stars for '94 are auspicious. Other short stories of mine have been published in *Metropolitan* 1 and by *Onlywomen Press*.

Pat Winslow

I am 40 and live in Bolton with my partner Jan. I write mostly poetry and short stories and my work appears in *Beyond Paradise*, *Herzone* and *Crocus Five Women Poets*. I have a story in Onlywomen's *Unknown Territory* and am a regular contributor to several journals. When I am not writing I try to earn some money as the Writer in Residence for Blackburn and as a tutor for the WEA in Greater Manchester. Will they ever pay me on time? Answers please to the Co-op Bank on Balloon Street.

About Commonword...

Commonword is a not-for-profit community publishing co-operative, producing books by writers in the North West, and supporting and developing their work. In this way Commonword brings new writing to a wide audience.

In general, Commonword seeks to encourage the creative writing and publishing of the diverse groups in society who have lacked, or been excluded from the means of expression through the written word. Working class writers, black people, women, disabled people, lesbians and gay men all too often fall into this category.

To give writers the opportunity to develop their work in an informal setting, Commonword offers a variety of writers' workshops, such as Womanswrite, the Monday Night Group, Northern Gay writers and the Disabled Writers Workshop.

...and Cultureword

Cultureword, a part of Commonword, was established in 1986 as a centre for black creative writing in the North West. Since that time it has achieved rapid success in discovering, developing and promoting black writers. Cultureword organises black writers' workshops, poetry performances, residencies and training events.

Crocus is the imprint for books published by Commonword and Cultureword. *No Limits* is the seventeenth title to be published under the Crocus imprint.

Through Commonword's Writers Agency we can also arrange for writers to perform their work or facilitate creative writing workshops in schools or other settings.

In addition to writers' workshops and publishing, Commonword offers a Manuscript Reading Service to give constructive criticism, and can give information and advice to writers about writing and publishing opportunities.

Commonword is supported by: the Association of Greater Manchester Authorities, North West Arts Board and Manchester Central Grants Unit.

The Commonword offices are at Cheetwood House, 21 Newton Street, Manchester M1 1FZ. Our phone number is (061) 236 2773. We would like to hear from you.

Recent Crocus titles

Kiss

A vivid collection of modern love poetry by Asian, African and Chinese writers. By turns tender, political and sensuous, this book single-handedly takes love poetry into the twenty-first century.
'These pieces of work are a testimony to the fact that our humanity, despite efforts to distort and destroy it, will always take priority.' (Martin Glynn)
ISBN 0946745 21 8
Price £5.95 Pbk.

Crocus Five Women Poets

A showcase of poetry by Barbara Bentley, Marguerite Gazeley, Francis Nagle, Sheila Parry and Pat Winslow. These five women are quickly emerging as some of the most talented poets in recent years.
'Here are poems that tackle everything from domestic chores to international politics with grace, wit and assurance.' (Steve Waling, City Life)
ISBN 0 946745 16 1
Price £5.95 Pbk

Dancing on Diamonds

Poetry and short stories from thirty-six young writers. Lively and provocative.
'The past revisited, the future seen with hopeful vision and the anger of the innocent. A collection of contemporary thoughts by a new breed of contemporary writers - a real pleasure.' (Art Malik)
ISBN 0 946745 06 4
Price £5.95 Pbk

The Delicious Lie

This book marks the arrival of a fresh, highly talented new voice onto the British poetry scene.
'What a wonderful, wonderful slice of love and life this is. A gorgeous, scrumptious piece of poetic justice from new(ish) writer Georgina Blake.' (Nayaba Aghedo, City Life)
ISBN 0 946745 07 2
Price £4.95 Pbk

Rainbows In The Ice

This book of poetry demonstrates the wealth of creative talent that exists within the disabled community. A unique and memorable collection.
'An impressive anthology... It's good to read poets who remember that expressing and eliciting emotion are the centrepieces of writing effective poetry.' (Robert Hamberger, Mailout)
ISBN 0 946745 90 0
Price £4.50 Pbk

A Matter of Fat (First Edition)

This incisive and humorous novel follows the fortunes of Stella, the leader of 'Slim-Plicity', a commercial slimming club, and some of the club members. When a Fat Women's Support Group starts up nearby, complications soon follow...
'In A Matter of Fat, Ashworth has retained a wicked sense of humour, while raising some very important questions.' (New Woman)
'Sherry Ashworth writes with wit, compassion, excruciating honesty, and controlled, creative anger.' (Zoe Fairbairns, Everywoman)
ISBN 0 946745 95 1
Price £4.95 Pbk

Flame

A dual language book of poetry in English and Urdu by Asian writers. Love, home life, racism and other political issues are some of the areas explored by the fifteen talented poets in Flame. Translations are by Alishan Zaidi.
'One of the best collections of Asian poetry I have read.' (Kam Kaur, Eastern Eye)
'Powerful and distinctive...a pleasure to read.' (Shelley Khair, Yorkshire Artscene)
ISBN 0 946745 85 4
Price £4.50 Pbk

Herzone

Fantasy short stories by women. Ranging from science fiction, to 'twist in the tale' stories and mythical fantasies, this collection has something to delight and entertain everyone.
'There is nothing but pleasure to be gained from these tales.' (Manchester Evening News)
'A varied and satisfying collection.' (Zoe Fairbairns, Everywoman)
ISBN 0 946745 80 3
Price £4.50 Pbk

Beyond Paradise

An original collection of poetry that celebrates the vitality of gay and lesbian writing. Provocative, funny and touching, *Beyond Paradise* offers fresh perspectives on life in the '90s – and beyond!
'I promise you, once you've read it, you'll keep coming back for another little glimpse of life in the lesbian and gay lane.'(Scene Out)
'The tragic nature of human existence, the fun and joy of being alive are here...' (Gay Times)
ISBN 0 946745 75 7
Price £4.50 Pbk

Relative to Me...

Short stories on family life. Families can be a source of inspiration – or desperation! The stories in *Relative to Me...* show both, with a wonderful mix of serious and light-hearted writing.
'Relative to Me... proves there's plenty of talent just waiting to burst forth from the region.' (Manchester Metro News)
'Twenty refreshingly original tales.' (The Teacher)
ISBN 0 946745 70 6
Price £3.95 Pbk

Talkers Through Dream Doors

Fourteen talented Black women write about their lives in this collection of poetry and short stories.
'These voices reassert the Black identity and cross new boundaries to redefine it.' (Amrit Wilson)
ISBN 0 946745 60 9
Price £3.50 Pbk

Now Then

Poetry and short stories illustrating lifestyles, work and leisure from 1945 to the present day.
'An extremely poignant evocation of times and places that no longer exist.' (Eileen Derbyshire - Coronation Street's Emily Bishop)
ISBN 0 946745 55 2
Price £3.50 Pbk

Holding Out

Women's lives are portrayed with realism, frankness and fun in this excellent collection of twenty-one short stories.
'A combination which guarantees realism, frankness and fun. I recommend.' (Barbara Castle MEP)
ISBN 0 946745 30 7
Price £3.50 Pbk

Other titles from Commonword

Black and Priceless, poetry and short stories.
0 946745 45 5, £3.50
Between Mondays, poetry from the Monday Night Group.
0 946745 35 8, £2.50
Identity Magazine, poetry and articles by Asian and African-Caribbean writers. £0.95
Liberation Soldier, poetry by Joe Smythe.
0 946745 25 0, £2.50
Poetic Licence, poetry from Greater Manchester.
0 946745 40 4, £2.50
Turning Points, a Northern Gay Writers collection.
0 946745 20 X, £2.95

For a recent catalogue of all our titles, write to:
Crocus books/Commonword
Cheetwood House
21 Newton Street
Manchester M1 1FZ.

If you are visually impaired and would like this book or any of our other titles to be produced on audio-tape please contact us.

ORDER FORM

TITLE	QUANTITY	PRICE	AMOUNT
Kiss		£5.95	
Crocus Five Women Poets		£5.95	
Dancing on Diamonds		£5.95	
The Delicious Lie		£4.95	
Rainbows In The Ice		£4.50	
A Matter of Fat		£4.95	
Herzone		£4.50	
Flame		£4.50	
Beyond Paradise		£4.50	
Relative to Me...		£3.95	
Talkers Through Dream Doors		£3.50	
Now Then		£3.50	
Black and Priceless		£3.50	
Holding Out		£3.50	
Identity Magazine		£0.95	
Poetic Licence		£2.50	
Between Mondays		£2.50	
Liberation Soldier		£2.50	
Turning Points		£2.95	

TOTAL _____

Please send a cheque or postal order, made payable to Commonword Ltd, covering the purchase price plus 50p per book postage and packing.

NAME _____

ADDRESS_____

_____

_____ POSTCODE _____

Please return to: Commonword, Cheetwood House, 21 Newton Street, Manchester M1 1FZ.